BLEAK HOUSE BOOKS

MADISON | WISCONSIN

Published by Bleak House Books, an imprint of Big Earth Publishing

923 Williamson St.

Madison, WI 53703

ISBN: 1-932557-17-2

Library of Congress Control Number: 2005936203

Cover design and illustrations: Peter Streicher

Book design: Peter Streicher

Book illustrations: Jeff Fisher

For Ellen, SJ, and Ken

❊ The Goods ❊

BULLIES' PULPIT

DEAD MAN	Joseph Wallace
THE LAST PICK	Jason Starr
HOUSE ENVY	Naomi Rand

POETRY, EXISTENTIALISM, AND BOCCE

WAITING FOR GALLO	Charlie Stella
STONES	Ken Bruen
THE BOCCE BALL KING OF FARRAGUT ROAD	Robert Randisi

JUST OFF THE BOAT

SUNSET	SJ Rozan
HIT AND RUN	Glenville Lovell
KILLING O'MALLEY	Tony Spinosa

GOOD COPS, BAD COP

BRENDA, MY STAR	Jim Fusilli
RIGHT IS RIGHT	Gabriel Cohen
THE LAST HONEST MAN IN BROOKLYN	Michele Martinez

JUSTICE BROOKLYN STYLE

LOCATION, LOCATION, LOCATION	Peter Spiegelman
ALL BLEEDING STOPS...EVENTUALLY	Tim Sheard
BONESHAKER	Maggie Estep

NO JUSTICE IN BROOKLYN, EVER

STEP UP	Ralph Pezzullo
GOING, GOING, GONE	Peter Blauner

INTRODUCTION
Not New York. Brooklyn!

Let's get something straight from the get go: *Hard-Boiled Brooklyn* is not an homage to tough guy detectives. If that's what you're looking for, look somewhere else. What I'm talking about here, what these stories are about at their core, is the nature of the beast. The very soul of the Brooklynite is hard-boiled. You may be born soft or move to the borough soft, but you don't stay soft for long. Brooklyn is like a third parent, the tough-love one, the one who gives you the truth about how things really are, and not the way they should be. You don't adopt Brooklyn, Brooklyn adopts you. You can't live in the place very long and remain unchanged. Sorry, it just don't work that way. You can crack our shells, but nothing runs out. See, that's what I'm saying.

At Brooklyn College, I took a great many poetry courses. Had my parents been paying any attention, they would have been horrified. And rightly so. In subsequent years, when I've found myself working in the cargo area at Kennedy Airport or driving a gypsy cab or selling cars or tending bar or waiting tables or hauling home heating oil, it has dawned on me that the occasional computer science class might have been a better idea than, let's say, *Poetry of the English Renaissance.* It took me years to get over my addiction to metaphysical conceits. But it was in one of these less than practical classes, *Romantic Poetry,* that the germ of this anthology was born.

That there is almost no mention of love in Romantic poetry may or may not be a revelation to you. It is nonetheless true. When we talk of romance as it relates to Romantic poetry, we are talking in terms of the long ago, the far away, and the exotic. For my money and by that definition, there's no more romantic place on earth than Brooklyn. For even when I lived there, even when I was part of it, the place and its inhabitants defied reason. While it is possible to know aspects of Brooklyn, it is folly to believe you can know it all, let alone explain it. Just try explaining why there are no eggs in egg creams.

Coney Island, Red Hook, Gravesend, Sheepshead Bay, Bushwick, Bed-Stuy, Cobble Hill, Brighton Beach, Canarsie, Brownsville—the mere mention of its neighborhoods conjures up all manner of wild images. As a kid growing up on Ocean Parkway in the shadow of Coney Island Hospital, I was aware there were neighborhoods in the borough as foreign to me as any small village in Asia and seemingly as exotic as Xanadu. But danger is the B-side, the dark underbelly, the unspoken undercurrent of exotic. The unknown, real or imagined, is always a threat. The foreign, the alien take us out of our comfort zones, wreak havoc on our equilibrium. And it is just that sort of discomfort—sometimes jarring and violent—that I was hoping for in the stories I solicited for this anthology, the kind of stories that test both the characters on the page and the readers.

With one or two exceptions, the contributors to *Hard-Boiled Brooklyn* were either born in, raised in, lived in, or worked in Brooklyn. Some, like me, have long since moved away, but the place stays with you. It persists as a state of mind. For me, the move away cemented the bond. Romance, as is its nature, increases with distance and time. It is not so much that my heart grew fonder as much as emptier. In my writing, in my life, I have struggled to find the place that ceased to exist the moment I left it. *How existential, huh?* Reading and editing this collection has given me insight into how other people struggle with the Brooklyn of the mind or the Brooklyn they've recently discovered.

I don't want to give you the wrong idea. I'm not one of the world's great planners or outliners. In fact, I pitched this anthology to Bleak House on the spur of the moment on my cell phone during a trip into Manhattan on the Long Island Railroad. At lunch that same day I asked roughly half of the writers whose stories appear in these pages if they would be interested in contributing to the collection. It was on the strength of their answers that the project was green-lighted. My instructions to the contributing authors was very spare indeed: A dark story of approximately twenty-five hundred words that screams Brooklyn. That was it. If the stories have a rough symmetry or if certain themes emerge, it's to Brooklyn's credit, not mine.

Here's a test. Next time you're traveling and you hear someone speaking with what you think is a Brooklyn accent, ask the speaker if he or she is from New York. If they say yes, that wasn't a Brooklyn accent.

—Reed Farrel Coleman, Editor

BULLIES'
PULPIT

DEAD MAN
by Joseph Wallace

"Be a man," Carl's friends told him.

Easy for them to say. Stew might push them into the Connells' hedge or against the Silvers' Lincoln Continental every once in a while, but that was no match for what he did to Carl.

And anyway, Carl *wasn't* a man, not yet. He was small and skinny, with flat feet so he ran funny, and weak arms so he threw like a girl.

How could he be a man?

"Figure something out," his friends said.

So Carl made a plan.

⬇

"Jesus," Stew said. "Look at this. The dirty little hole where the freak hides."

"You can't come in here," Carl said. He was crouched down in the half-darkness, taking in great gulps of the cool air. His palms were flat on the ground, the dirt and rocks cold under his fingers. "This is *my* place."

"Yeah?" Stew squatted, letting out a comfortable groan. He was barely out of breath. "You know something? I don't think so."

Then, with a flick of one thick wrist, he backhanded Carl across the face. Carl felt something tear in his neck as his head jerked backwards. His mouth and cheek went numb, but he could taste the blood dripping from his split upper lip.

Even in the dim light, he could see that Stew wasn't done, wasn't even close to being done. He was grinning and flexing his fingers, and Carl knew exactly what *that* meant.

So he grabbed the chunk of concrete and swung it as hard as he could at Stew's head.

Having pictured this moment in his mind a thousand times.

↯

The grown-ups had no clue. To them, one block of Midwood was much like another. Whether you were on East Twenty-first Street between Avenues L and M, or Twenty-fourth Street between O and P, you lived on a street lined with two-story wood-frame houses built in the 1920s. Some were finished in stucco, others in aluminum siding, but each had a postage-stamp lawn, a garage, a tree, well-tended flower beds, and either a young couple raising their children or an older one lamenting the passing of the good old days.

But the kids on East Twenty-first Street knew the truth. Every one of them understood exactly where the borderlines were.

Their real neighborhood, they knew, was actually barely larger than the block they lived on. Head down East Twenty-first across Avenue M, for example, and you were unlikely to make it back alive. Crazy old Mr. Feldman lived there, the guy who shot pigeons from his front porch and threatened to shoot you.

Go the other way, and you couldn't even cross Avenue L. Teenagers drag-raced there, and a six-year-old, wandering away from his mother's eye and out into the street, had been run over and killed in broad daylight just last year. It was off-limits, and Mrs. Milner on the corner made sure you didn't try to sneak across.

You could go as far east as Twenty-third Street, but only if you kept your eyes out, because that was part of the territory of that big guy who lived on Bedford Avenue, Terry or Perry or something. You were almost guaranteed to get beaten up if he or his friends—his *slaves*—saw you.

Your best shot was west. You could walk along Avenue M, where the stores and restaurants were, all the way down to the el station at Sixteenth Street, so long as you stayed with the crowds of old ladies and moms pushing baby carriages. But just half a block away, the side streets were empty of all but garbage that swirled up into little tornadoes in the wind, and people—adults, not kids—ready to mug you for whatever you carried. Some coins, a bottle of Coke, a comic book.

Dangers abounded outside the narrow borders of the neighborhood. But stay where you belonged, and you'd be safe.

Unless Stew decided he didn't like you.

Then no place was safe.

🌿

"Fight back."

That's what Carl's friends said, though Carl noticed that none of them ever volunteered to help.

"Don't put up with it," they said. "Fight back. That's the only way to deal with bullies."

But they're bigger than me, Carl told them. And there's four of them.

"But Stew's the boss."

Obviously.

"You take care of him, the rest will leave you alone."

This was probably true too.

"The one thing you can't do is just sit back and take it," Carl's friends said. "You have to stand up for yourself."

Be a man.

🌿

They were up against the closed door of Snider's Delicatessen, Carl with his back against the iron grating, Stew in his face, his guys, Pete and Hank and Rob, crowding around, getting a close look while blocking the view of any potential do-gooder who might walk past.

Not that there was much chance of that. It was Saturday, late in the afternoon, and with the sky rumbling with thunder and all the Jewish stores closed, Avenue M was a lot less crowded than usual. Carl wouldn't normally have ventured out under such risky conditions, but today he had his plan.

Of course there were some grown-ups around, even now. But so what? What good did that do? Grown-ups almost never paid attention to what kids were doing anyway—or if they noticed, they just didn't care. They were as likely to yell at Carl for getting hit as they were at Stew for doing the hitting.

Stew had one forearm against Carl's throat, and in his other hand he held Carl's right wrist. Carl saw how fragile his wrist looked, as if all Stew had to do was twist and the flesh would fall off like overcooked chicken meat sagging away from the bone.

"Stewed chicken," Carl said out loud, without thinking.

Stew leaned in closer. Carl knew every pimple, every freckle of that pale-skinned face, the snubby, upturned nose, the fine reddish hairs on the upper lip, the way the blue eyes seemed to darken when they had Carl in their sights.

"What did you say?" Stew asked.

But Carl just shook his head.

Stew nodded. "Okay, don't tell me." He leaned harder, pressing with his forearm until little sparks swam around in front of Carl's eyes. Only when Carl's head sagged did he pull back, a little.

Carl took some deep breaths, struggling to get the air down into his lungs. Then he leaned his head back against the grating, the metal smelling of rust and pastrami and dog pee. "Why?" he asked.

Stew blinked. Then his upper lip lifted, revealing the snaggled front tooth that was the first thing most people noticed about him. "Because I want to," he said, as if explaining the obvious to a retard.

Because I can.

Of course. It had been a stupid question. Bullies don't need a reason. They can ruin your life just because they don't like the look of your face.

Carl opened his mouth to say something—at least talking delayed the inevitable—but Stew leaned harder. The sparks swam. "Also, my hands get all itchy," he added. "They need something to do."

He let go for a second to look down at his hands; large, hairless, pinkish-white in the warm sun. He moved his fingers around like a spider's legs, then raised his eyes to make sure Carl was watching too.

That's when Carl reached back and hit him in the stomach.

Stew made a sound like a seal barking and doubled over. Before the other boys could react, Carl pushed his way through them and took off.

Praying he'd get enough of a lead before Stew came after him. But not too much of one.

"You're a dead man, asshole," Stew called after him.

Not this time, Carl thought.

☙

No: There was one safe place.

Carl called it the Tunnel, but it was really just a gap between two garages, the Hanlons' and the Segals', whose houses were across the street from Carl's. Two garages built at the same time, identical except that the Hanlons' had a blue door and the Segals' a red one.

The Tunnel's opening was maybe ten or twelve inches across, far too small for any adult to enter, but easy for Carl when he was little and still just big enough for him this summer.

For six years he'd been coming here. Venturing inside only when no one was around, the dads away at work, the moms off shopping. He knew how fragile it was, this refuge, how easily denied to him, the only place on Twenty-first Street where someone's eyes weren't always on you.

Too soon and he'd outgrow it. But not quite yet.

To enter the Tunnel, he had to turn sideways and shuffle along, the rough concrete outer walls of the two garages scraping against his skin, the overlapping edges of the roofs overhead blocking out the light. Spiderwebs would cling to his face, and once a bat came hurtling past, inches above his head, and blundered out into the sunlight behind him. Stones and bits of concrete and dry old leaves would crunch under his feet.

At the very back, the gap widened a bit into what Carl called the Chamber. Back here in the dimness, the only light coming from the entrance fifteen feet away, Carl could sit in safety amid old bricks and chunks of concrete, resting his back against the cold cinderblocks someone had stacked to keep the passage from leading into the backyard of a house on East Twenty-second Street. His only company, pillbugs and centipedes and daddy longlegs, and that's the way he wanted it.

Here, with a flashlight, he'd play out chess games from a book on a little magnetic board he'd gotten with his allowance money, or read the mysteries and science-fiction novels that were his favorites. Robert Heinlein and Raymond Chandler and Dick Francis, books with men in them who might not be the biggest and strongest people in the world, but who always ended up fighting back.

Who always figured something out.

Afterwards, as usual, the grown-ups didn't come within a mile of guessing the truth. If they'd spent any time paying attention to their kids, if they'd ever bothered to look at what was going on right in plain sight, they'd have been onto it in a minute. But of course they hadn't.

The kids in the neighborhood, though, *they* knew. They couldn't figure out exactly what had happened, or how it had happened, but they knew who was responsible.

Pete, Hank, and Rob, the rest of the old gang, never went near him again. They stopped hanging out on Twenty-first Street, and pretty soon they didn't spend much time together at all. As if they were afraid that being in a group made them more vulnerable, more likely to be next.

As soon as they were old enough, they left Midwood forever. It was what local kids did anyway when they grew up, leave, but those three were in a special hurry.

And they never came back.

⚜

All four of them chased him, but Hank and Pete and Rob gave up soon. It had begun to rain, hard, so why get wet, when they'd have plenty of chances to torment him in the future? Hey—they knew where he lived. Where was he gonna go?

Carl turned onto Twenty-first Street. As the rain came down harder, he saw people running for their front doors. He knew that the Hanlons were away for the weekend, the Segals spending the day visiting their cousins in Queens. Except for old Mrs. Milner, humping her groceries along down by the far corner, the sidewalks were deserted.

The dark stripe of the Tunnel opened before him.

Just as he turned sideways to edge his way in, he heard a laugh. Stew was standing there, right behind him, arms crossed, bouncing on his feet, drenched to the skin but not caring. His eyes were wide with understanding.

"So *that's* where you disappear to," Stew said.

He took a step closer. "I mean, where you *used* to disappear to."

Carl looked at him for a moment, then continued on, faster than usual, his cheeks scraping against the rough stone. He was panting so hard, almost gasping for air, he thought he might get stuck, but he finally made it into the Chamber.

He crouched at the far end, his back against the cinderblocks. The rain drummed down on the roofs above, an occasional drip making it through and thudding against the stony floor.

For fifteen seconds, half a minute, there was silence from out-side. Then Carl heard Stew's voice, and something blocked the light at the Tunnel's entrance.

"Maybe I'll just brick this up and leave you here to starve," Stew said.

Then he said, "Nah. My hands are itchy."

Carl reached down and picked up the chunk of concrete he'd chosen days ago. It fit as comfortably into his hand as if it had grown there.

"Jesus, this is tight," Stew said, edging his way forward. "I'll come back with dynamite and blast my way in, you fuck."

But he wasn't giving up. He was making his way through.

"Oh, you're dead," he said. "You're so dead."

This was his dream: Catching Carl in a place where there were no witnesses, from which there was no escape.

Then, with a last curse and grunt, he was inside the Chamber. He stood, backlit, his face in shadow as he looked around at the chessboard, the copy of *Stranger in a Strange Land*, the flashlight, the Tupperware container with Oreos in it.

"Look at this," he said in disgusted wonder. "The dirty little hole where the freak hides."

"You can't come in here," Carl told him. "This is *my* place."

⚐

The cops never thought to search there.

So typical. None of them could possibly fit into the Tunnel, so it didn't occur to them that someone else, someone smaller, might be able to.

He had run away, some speculated. After all, he was always an odd boy, that one.

He was abducted, others theorized. After all, New York City was a dangerous place.

No one ever mentioned bullies and their victims. The adults had never noticed, and the kids were smart enough—and scared enough—not to breathe a word of it.

So none of the leads panned out. And though the police promised the family that they were still actively pursuing the case, it was easy to tell they'd moved on to other things.

And if any odor ever escaped the cool, dry Chamber and made its way onto East Twenty-first Street, no one noticed or commented on it.

But it was unlikely that any ever did. It was a long way from the Chamber to the street.

And after all, Carl hadn't been a very big kid.

ꙮ

The chunk of concrete grazed the top of Stew's head before slipping from Carl's grasp. It struck the wall and bounced away, landing far out of reach.

There was complete silence as the two of them stared at each other, realizing at the same moment what was going to happen next.

Then Carl felt Stew's itchy hands around his throat, squeezing. He plucked at the fingers, at the thumbs that were crushing his Adam's apple, but he knew it was hopeless. As the sparks swam— then flew—in his head, his arms fell to his sides.

But before he went away he thought: I did what I was supposed to do. I stood up for myself. I fought back.

This must be what it feels like to be a man.

THE LAST PICK
by Jason Starr

"I GOT EVAN," ROB SAID.

Evan left the group of kids standing off to the side and joined Rob.

"Steve," Jimmy said.

Justin was pointing to himself, wanting Rob to pick him. Mike was looking down, trying not to be chosen. Jimmy and Mike were a great passing combination so Mike wanted to be on Jimmy's team.

"Mike," Rob said.

"Oh, man," Mike said.

Rob was smiling proudly.

Jimmy, looking serious, unfazed, said, "Justin."

Now there were only two guys left—me and Dave. Although Dave weighed about 150 pounds and couldn't run very well because of his asthma, it was obvious he would get picked ahead of me. I was always the last pick. Not only was I the smallest and thinnest guy on the block, I also had knock knees. This was back in the seventies, before orthotics, so I had to wear corrective shoes to help fix the problem. Kids made fun of me all the time for my shoes, calling me Herman Munster because of the way I clunked around when I ran. I was also very uncoordinated. I threw worse than most girls and I couldn't catch very well either. Although I'd been trying to get better at sports, throwing a Spalding against the wall at P.S. 152

every day during recess, I hadn't made any progress. Having me on a team was considered to be like playing one man short.

Rob was already smiling, knowing Jimmy would get stuck with me.

"I got the fatso," Rob said.

Dave went over next to Rob, nudging him in the side playfully.

Shaking his head, walking away, Jimmy said to me, "Come on, Spaz."

Rob led his team up the block to one sewer, and I followed Jimmy and my other teammates in the opposite direction, toward the other sewer.

My team huddled without me, but by the way the guys kept looking over at me, giggling, I knew I was the butt of some joke. I used to cry when kids teased me, but I'd become used to it. Since third grade kids had been picking on me, thanks to Jimmy. Before third grade I never had a problem with him. In kindergarten we were even friends and I used to go over to his house to play sometimes. But for some reason, in the third grade, he started hating me. On the first day of school, when I had to get up in front of the class and talk about what I did for my summer vacation, he threw a spit ball and hit me right in the forehead. The teacher yelled at him but he didn't even get punished. He continued teasing and tormenting me every day and, because he was the most popular kid in school, other kids started hating me too. It wasn't so bad when Jimmy wasn't around—the time he was out of school for a week with chicken pox was heaven for me—but when he was around my life was pure hell. Usually, I tried to avoid him as much as possible, staying inside every day after school and watching TV by myself. But sometimes I got lonely and went out to play with him and the guys anyway, hoping things would change.

The huddle broke up. Jimmy pointed his index finger at me and warned, "You better not touch the ball."

My team spread out to receive the throw off. I drifted far back behind them. Naturally, Rob, who had a great arm, threw the ball right at me. Jimmy yelled for me to get out of the way, but my reaction time was slow and by the time I spotted the ball in the air and judged that it would reach me, it was too late to avoid it. Just as I was starting to run away the ball hit me in the middle of the back.

"Ow!" It hurt like hell.

Mike, from Rob's team, who was the fastest runner on the block, recovered the fumble in our end zone for a touchdown.

Guys on Rob's team were laughing and my teammates were calling me "doofus" and "spaz."

My back was still stinging when Jimmy came over to me and pushed me so hard I almost fell down.

"What the hell's wrong with you? I told you not to touch the ball."

"Sorry," I said.

"You're such a retard. Why were you even born?"

I wanted to talk back to him, but then I remembered the last time I'd talked back to him. It was at school, in the auditorium, when we were getting ready to watch *The Red Balloon*. Jimmy was teasing me and I called him a stupid idiot, and he punched me as hard as he could, right in my gut. This time, I guess I did the smart thing and I kept my mouth shut.

Justin came over and said to Jimmy, "Leave him alone, man."

Justin was my best friend. Well, he used to be my best friend, until he became friends with Jimmy, so he couldn't be friends with me anymore. Still, Justin was never mean to me. Like everybody else, he joined in laughing sometimes when Jimmy picked on me, but he never teased me on his own.

"He's gonna lose the game for us," Jimmy said.

"No, he won't," Justin said. "Come on, let's just play."

"Car!" Rob called out.

Everyone stood off to the sides, in front of the parked cars, as the car sped down East Twenty-fourth Street.

The teams lined up for the next throw off. Jimmy instructed me to stand right behind him this time so there was no way I could touch the ball.

Rob threw the ball right at us, slightly over our heads. Jimmy pushed me back with his ass, knocking me to the street, and then he backed up and caught the ball. He took a few steps and then was two-hand touched.

The game continued. On offense, Jimmy didn't pass the ball to me, even though the other team didn't even bother defending me and I was always wide open. On defense, I counted Mississippis, which meant I pretty much didn't have to do anything. Whenever it was our team's turn to receive a throw off, Jimmy made sure I didn't touch the ball or do anything to hurt the team.

We were losing 35–28 when Rob and Jimmy decided that the first team to 42 would be the winner. It was third down and we were practically an entire sewer away from scoring a touchdown. My team huddled with me standing off to the side.

Then Jimmy said, "Hey, Spaz, get over here!"

I came over cautiously, afraid it was a trick and Jimmy would punch me in the gut.

"This is what we're gonna do." Jimmy looked at Steve and Justin. "You two go to the red van and stop there for a second. Then I'm gonna yell 'Go deep!' and you run to the end zone. I'll look like I'm gonna throw the ball to one of you guys, then I'll throw it to Spaz."

"Yeah, right," Steve said.

"Shut up and listen to me," Jimmy said. "This is gonna work. Nobody'll ever expect me to throw it to him." Jimmy turned to me. "You're just gonna stand like five feet in front of me. All you gotta do is catch the ball—just catch it, then lateral it right back to me. Just a little lateral and I'll run for the TD."

"Come on, that won't work," Justin said.

"Yes it will," Jimmy said. Then he said to me, "You better not mess up."

We went to the line of scrimmage. When Jimmy said, "Hut" and received the snap I was so nervous I suddenly had to pee. For once in my life, I wanted to do something well in sports. I wanted to make a big play and have my team swarm around me and say, "Nice going," or "All right."

I went to the spot where I was supposed to go and turned around and faced Jimmy.

"Go deep!" Jimmy yelled.

Steve and Justin sprinted toward the end zone.

Jimmy faked throwing a long bomb, and then lobbed the ball to me. It was an easy pass to catch. I was watching the ball all the way and was ready to grab it out of the air. But then I started thinking about everyone watching me, expecting me to screw up, getting ready to laugh. Maybe I blinked or just took my eye off the ball for a second because my hands came together too late when the ball had already bounced off my chest and onto the ground.

As I'd expected, the laughter and teasing came. I just stood there, hating myself.

"Man, what the hell's wrong with you?" Jimmy said. He picked up the football and drilled it at me, hitting me right in the ass.

"Ow!" I shouted.

The laughter and teasing got even louder. Even Justin was joining in.

"Going or throwing?" Rob asked.

"Throwing," Jimmy said.

As my team lined up for the throw off, I glared at Jimmy. I was probably thinking about a lot of things right then, but I was mainly thinking about all the times Jimmy had tormented me, making my life hell. I was thinking about the time he spat in my face in the back of Mrs. Klein's class last year, the time he whacked me in my back with a Whiffle ball bat and gave me a big welt, the time he stole my parka from my cubby and I had to walk home in the freezing cold and got tonsillitis. Then there were the other, countless times, he'd called me names or punched me or did whatever else he could think of to hurt me and humiliate me.

"Hey, Spaz," Jimmy called out. "You coming over here or what?"

I walked over there slowly, not taking my eyes off him.

"What're you looking at, Spaz?"

I didn't say anything.

Jimmy threw the ball to Rob's team and they went on offense. I did my job, counting Mississippis, but I felt like I wasn't even there. I was somewhere else, wishing I had a way to get back at Jimmy, make him pay once and for all for all the bad things he'd done to me.

Rob's team didn't score and we got the ball back. My team huddled without me and Jimmy connected on a couple of passes to Justin. Then Jimmy threw a touchdown pass to Steve and the score was tied, 35–35.

"Baby!" Jimmy shouted. He high-fived with Steve and Justin in the end zone. "One more TD and we win. If it wasn't for the Spaz we woulda won already."

Jimmy, Justin, and Steve lined up for the throw off. Jimmy saw me lagging behind.

"Come on, get over here. What the hell's wrong with you?"

I drifted over toward Jimmy.

"Car! Justin yelled.

Everyone stood to the sides as the car sped down the block. I was standing between two parked cars and Jimmy was right in front of me, so close I could see the sweat on the back of his neck. Maybe it was all the hate in me building up, giving me the strength to finally do something about it. Or maybe I was just sick of keeping my mouth shut, of taking it. Whatever it was, I suddenly felt different, stronger, and I knew exactly what I had to do.

The car was getting closer. I was between the cars so nobody saw me push Jimmy. He was so much bigger than me, it took all my might, strength I didn't even know I had. He stumbled a few feet forward and the car slammed into him. It happened so fast, I don't think he ever had any idea how or why he was being crushed to death.

Afterward, it was chaos—kids screaming, neighbors rushing out. Jimmy's parents weren't home, but his housekeeper was there, crying. Then the ambulance and cops came.

All the kids were questioned, including me. I told the same story that everyone else did, that Jimmy must've tripped and fallen in front of the car, or the car had swerved slightly and hit him. The driver of the car—a hysterical woman—was eventually questioned, but she wasn't drunk and the death was ruled an accident. No one ever suspected I was involved. I guess no one could've even imagined that a spaz like me would have the guts to do something like that to a kid like Jimmy.

All the attention Jimmy got after his death was very annoying. At school, there was a big memorial for him in the auditorium and all of the teachers and students attended. I had to wear a suit and a tight tie that hurt my neck. Because my mother knew Jimmy's mother from the PTA, I had to hear Jimmy's name over and over again at home, and I had to hear people around the neighborhood talking about how sad and awful it was that he was dead. I even had to go to the funeral.

But, after awhile, all the fuss blew over. Jimmy's family moved away, people stopped talking about him in school and around the neighborhood—it was as if *he'd* never been born. Meanwhile, my life improved drastically. I went to school every day without having to worry about getting beaten up and humiliated. My knees got better and I didn't have to wear corrective shoes anymore. Without Jimmy around, kids stopped picking on me and I started making friends. I developed more self-confidence, grew a few inches, and didn't look as awkward. I would never be a great athlete, but I started wearing the right clothes and listening to the right music and, by junior high, I was considered to be one of the cool guys in the neighborhood. Even girls started liking me.

I've never had any regrets about what I did to Jimmy that day. But, sometimes, when I think about all the time he stole from me, the chunk of my childhood he took away that I can never get back, I just wish I'd gotten rid of him a lot sooner.

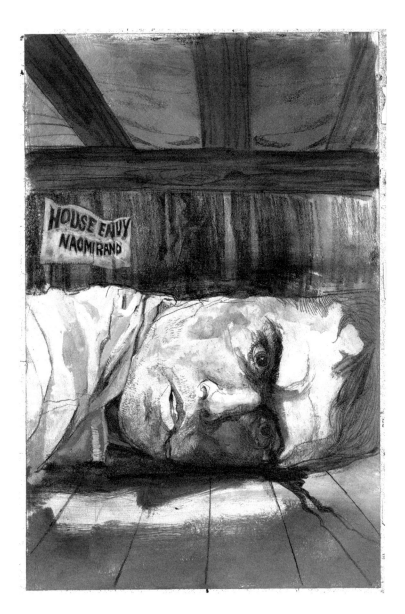

HOUSE ENVY
NAOMI RAND

IT WAS HIM AGAIN, RUDY, THE TENANT from hell. Arlene shoved the pillow over her head. But it was no use. That pale white finger was glued to the buzzer. If she didn't let him in, he would call from his cell phone, and if she refused to lift the phone, he'd simply call back again and again and again. If she turned off the ringer, he'd start howling like a wolf.

He'd done that last night, waking the neighbors.

She couldn't chance it.

Arlene sat up slowly, then tried to lift herself. Eight and a half months pregnant, but who was counting? Me, Arlene thought. All her friends had claimed it would get easier after the first trimester. But the nausea had only gotten worse, and the exhaustion was literally mind numbing. Her legs were swollen. It was a victory when she stood. Arlene managed to get out of bed, and veered across the room, getting to the window. She held onto the frame for ballast and righted herself like the great ocean liner she was. Make that, Arlene thought, a cruise ship; one where the passengers and crew had contracted salmonella.

The buzzer bleated.

"Jesus!"

Arlene didn't bother with the lights, she could see fine, there was a streetlamp directly in front of her window. The first week here on Bergen, she'd been unable to bear the light shining in, and they'd put up heavy curtains, but later on, she'd kept them open just enough to find her way. She didn't really like it when it was so dark you couldn't see in front of you, which was how it was back where she'd grown up, in a small town in Indiana. The closest city was over two hours away. When she went to bed, as a child, and her mother shut the door, it was easy to imagine bad things happening, witches flying down from the ceiling to steal her soul, or axe murderers hiding in the corner, waiting for her mother's footsteps to recede.

Here, you could always see what was going on, and even late at night there were people to be found. Sometimes, lying in bed, when she couldn't sleep, she'd hear snippets of their conversations.

It was two flights down from her bedroom to the ground floor of the four-story red brick house. She paused before opening the door and heard Rudy, outside, offering a running commentary on her shortcomings. "Motherfuckingbitchcuntwhore."

Arlene was tall, big boned, her mother used to say; she'd been captain of the girls' basketball team at her high school, and she'd gone to Indiana U on an athletic scholarship. At first, she'd thought that that was what she'd do because she was only a kid and what did she really know, but then she'd torn her Achilles tendon and discovered that she had a head for math, for statistics really, and that was how she ended up majoring in business. She'd met her husband Bart (yes short for Bartholomew) on campus; he was pre-law. When they graduated they both got into Columbia and so they moved to the big city to start their new life. Somehow Brooklyn was not part of the fantasy.

Standing just on the other side of the heavy wooden door, Arlene thought that if Bart had been home, he'd be down here, dealing with Rudy. But he was in Italy, working on a bankruptcy case. He'd felt guilty about leaving, considering, but what choice did he have if he wanted to make partner?

Arlene rolled the tumblers. Pulling the door open she backed up quickly. If she didn't, he'd slam it into her as he shoved through. "Lost my keys," he muttered.

"Again?"

He'd been losing them consistently every night for the last month. Irony was lost on him. Rudy staggered over to his apartment, opened the door, and slammed it shut against inquiring eyes.

Arlene looked out at Bergen Street. What a peaceful block this was, the brownstones and brick homes dark, the stoops bare. A car roared by. In the distance a siren wailed. Shutting the door, she regretfully clicked the lock, knowing that there were only two people inside the house now. She could hear Rudy's progress through his garden apartment, furniture being shoved aside as he made his way into the bedroom. Arlene checked her glow in the dark watch. 3:28.

Back upstairs she chose the living room as sanctuary. But that was no good, she could hear him snoring, right through the wooden floorboards.

How had she let this happen? No, Arlene corrected herself, how had they?

They'd overpaid for the house for one thing. And then, the closing had been put off, and off interminably, so that when they finally moved in, they'd been desperate, having packed their things and rented a place at outrageous expense on a week-to-week basis, thinking that it wouldn't be necessary to stay. They'd advertised the rental in the *Times*, and Rudy had been their first applicant. He'd worn a gray suit and matching tie, and introduced the woman who came with him as his fiancée. He'd written down references for them. And they'd done their best to check, calling his place of employment. They'd spoken with his supposed boss. They hadn't done exhaustive research; she was already six months pregnant by then, and he'd seemed so nice.

Such a nice young couple, Arlene thought. She braved a smile. A week after he moved in his rent check bounced. That was when they discovered his job was about as fictitious as the fiancée who they'd never set eyes on again. God knew where she'd come from. Perhaps they'd met at Cody's over on Court Street. Or at Cousins. Those seemed to be his two favorite local drinking establishments.

Arlene climbed upstairs to the baby's room. It was freshly painted. They'd set up the crib they'd bought at Jacadi, next to it the prim blue and white striped rug and the black and white mobile, designed especially to stimulate a newborn's IQ. She pushed on it, gently, just as the baby began to hammer its feet against her stomach.

Their house was in Boerum Hill, a neighborhood that was outrageously expensive, despite the housing projects only a block away. The realtor had claimed the white apartment buildings that towered over the rest of the neighborhood were about to be turned into co-ops. After they'd paid $1.7 million dollars for their home, they discovered that realtors had been feeding unsuspecting clients that story for the last fifteen years. It was as much an urban legend as the poodle in the microwave. Still, the neighborhood seemed safe enough; on Smith Street old mom-and-pop hardware stores and a Met that had produce from before the Great Depression were bounded by hip bars, clothing stores, and some of the city's best restaurants.

They liked it here. Of course the house had been a stretch, but when Bart made partner in April of next year, they'd be set.

Arlene stroked the baby's comforter. It was her favorite, a soothing patchwork of animals in light pink and soft blue. They hadn't wanted to learn the sex; Bart liked surprises. They couldn't decide on the names; for a girl Bart wanted his grandmother's Delia, if it was a boy, Edward. She disagreed, but quietly.

They'd so wanted this child. She'd had trouble getting pregnant, and miscarried twice, but this time round, everything was fine. Everything that is, except for Rudy.

They'd assumed they could just throw him out. But it turned out that they were mistaken. Even though he'd bounced rent check after rent check, getting rid of him would require going to court, and that would take up to a year. Once they did get a judgment, (assuming it was in their favor), it would take even more time to actually get him physically off the premises. As for changing the lock and throwing him out on the street, that was the worst thing they could do. He could sue them then and he'd win.

In fact, it was Rudy who'd changed the locks, the ones on the door of his apartment; he said he didn't want them snooping around.

He had them, as her mom liked to say, 'over a barrel.' Not a position she felt comfortable with, considering her current heft. Then she felt it. The building was shaking. The bastard wasn't asleep after all.

Salsa. It was what he loved to blare, this pale, red-haired white male.

They'd tried calling the police the first few times he woke them with his music, but when and if they did show up, he'd lower the volume and act completely meek and submissive, then as soon as they'd driven away, he'd turn it up several notches more to punish them.

There was a limit, Arlene told herself. There would have to be. This couldn't go on. The baby was almost here and what then? But of course Bart was gone till Saturday.

Arlene couldn't help thinking that it was Bart who had gotten them into this mess in the first place. Bart who wouldn't even consider bribing him to leave. "I'll be damned if he's going to get the better of us," Bart had said.

Arlene didn't point out the obvious, that he already had.

Arlene decided she was going to have to take matters into her own hands. She was going to have to find out what it would take to get him out of there and do it herself before Bart returned. If it led to a fight, so be it. Truthfully though, Arlene thought, Bart would make a show of how she should have waited for him, but he'd actually be relieved.

Arlene went down the first set of stairs, and the music got louder, down the second set and it was ear shattering. Inside that door, she imagined Rudy prancing to the Latin beat. She banged with an open hand. No response. How could he hear her, and even if he did, he would ignore her. Arlene got pen and paper and wrote a simple question, then slid it under the door.

How much do you want?

In the morning, Arlene woke to the alarm bleary eyed. Coffee disagreed with her. So there was no relief to be had from this brain-damaged state. As she stepped across the threshold, to get her home-delivered *New York Times*, she saw her slip of paper, with an answer scrawled on the bottom.

20,000 dollares

Was the spelling supposed to indicate his preferred ethnicity? And more to the point, would he accept a check?

They certainly didn't have the cash available. They had all of three thousand dollars in their combined savings and checking accounts. What money they'd saved had gone to the down payment. They'd assumed a preposterously high level of debt, believing the realtor when she told them that the rental payments would cover the differential. Arlene realized that it would cost much less money to take out a contract on Rudy. And it would be a whole lot more gratifying, besides.

Arlene worked at an investment firm in downtown Manhattan. She had found it exciting at first, but over time, there was a sameness to the job. Her clients cared about one thing, and one thing only: the growth of their money. Which was as it should be, she noted, only once she got pregnant she discovered that she hated them for it. She, who had always loved what money could buy, actually felt their concerns to be petty and beneath them.

What was that, she wondered? Hormones?

Bart phoned her just after she got in that morning.

"How are you doing?" he asked.

"Fine."

"Did he bother you last night?"

"No," she lied. Because what was the point of saying anything else? "How's Milan?"

"I wish I could tell you, we've been cooped up in here for days." Of course it was just after three Italian time, and she heard male laughter in the background. "Have to go," he said. "I would have called last night when I got back to the room, but it was so late; the meetings went on till eleven, and then there was dinner with the client. I was beat." He lowered his voice, adding, "I love you."

"Love you too," she said.

When Rudy buzzed that night, Arlene was dreaming that the buzzer meant she should abandon ship. She ran down the dark, smoke-infested corridors, but there was no way out. Then, still asleep, she realized what it was, and roused herself.

When she opened the downstairs door, Rudy was too fast for her. As he barged through, he shoved her back into the wall. Alcohol fumes rose off of him in waves.

"Thanks a bunch," he said, and giggled. "So, you got my money?"

"Not quite yet," she told him.

"Not quite yet?" He was mimicking her. Then he was gone. Arlene heard him scuttling round behind the wall, like the rat he was.

In the morning, she called in sick. Then she opened the Brooklyn Yellow Pages.

Arlene walked up Bergen to the F train stop. She took the F train heading for Coney Island. Although they had a car, she decided it was better to take the subway. Somehow it was suitably anonymous for the task at hand. She'd never gone in this direction before, and was surprised when, only a few minutes later, the train pulled up into daylight. Looking out, she saw small buildings stretching off into the distance, some with old style laundry lines with clothing drying on them. Her mother had a set of six in their backyard. Growing up, she'd loved pressing her face into the sheets; there was something soothing in the odor they gave off as they dried out in the sun.

At Fort Hamilton Parkway she got off and checked the map, then walked the three blocks to AJ Supply. Inside, there were racks of distressed blue jeans and blotchy one-piece camouflage jumpsuits. In her condition, Arlene had a hard time moving through the over-stuffed racks. At the very back of the store, there were locked glass cases. One held hunting rifles, another handguns, a third, knives and a fourth, samurai swords.

"Name's Mickey. So, beautiful, what can I do you for?"

Arlene turned to find the man had snuck up on her. He had on fatigues and a cap that read USMC. He looked at most twenty-five. The moustache above his pink and fleshly upper lip looked like a chubby black caterpillar.

"I'm thinking of buying my husband a present," Arlene said, watching as he took in her *condition*. She'd morphed from potentially sexual to someone who was out of the question and even vaguely disgusting.

"What's he into?"

She pointed to the case that held the handguns.

In the end though, she had to settle. There was a waiting period for the handguns, and a license as well. And even then, there was no guarantee that you'd be approved, or so he explained. So Arlene had him put the air rifle in an oversized shopping bag, after wrapping it with brown paper to avoid prying eyes. She also invested in a switchblade and a can of mace. He called her a car service to get home.

Arlene set the box on the rosewood dining room table, the one they'd bought at Scott Jordan. She cracked it open and loaded it with pellets. She herself had had a BB gun, but she'd only used it for target practice. Her brother, on the other hand, had shot at anything that moved. Later on, his hobbies turned to getting drunk and stoned on the weekends, and then he got his high-school girlfriend pregnant and settled down. He sold Fords at the local dealership. He liked to say, "I do all right for myself."

Back then, though, he'd grab the BB gun away, then whip it round and aim it at her.

She had never liked him. Was it wrong to feel that way about your brother? Would her own child feel that way, if he or she had siblings? Arlene hoped not.

Lifting the air gun she looked through the sight. She imagined Rudy crossing the street in front of her, and her finger caressed the trigger. Then setting it down on the table again, she climbed the stairs to the spare room where they kept the things they had no use for. In the corner were the tools; hammers, nails, screwdrivers, and a small hacksaw.

She took the hammer and screwdriver and went downstairs to Rudy's apartment. Knocking hard, she waited. Then tried again. When she was sure he wasn't in, she pulled up the plates of the locks, and unscrewed the cylinders, then turned the knob. The door swung open. Stepping inside, she remembered the realtor showing off this rental apartment, the quaint woodstove in the living room, the lovely garden view. Bart had been the one who had said that they'd look for a nice young couple, and maybe they even would want to baby-sit. In his mind, he must have thought they would become one loving, extended family. Only two of the four would be paying for the privilege.

Rudy's living room was furnished with a gray Barcalounger easy chair held together with duct tape and a widescreen plasma TV. Looking through to the bedroom she saw that the bed was unmade and on the floor next to it were piles of dirty clothes. There was a milk carton doubling as a side table. On it was mail, looking closer she saw it was a pile of unpaid bills. In the closet were two suits, one she recognized as the disguise he'd worn on the day they'd met.

The kitchen was stocked with those plastic glasses you got free from McDonald's. In the fridge he'd set a container of milk and leftovers from various take-out orders. She had a momentary surge of pity. Then she shook it off. Moved back to the living room, and stood the perfect distance away, then swung the hammer round like mighty Thor, smashing the TV screen.

Afternoon stretched into evening. Arlene sat in her living room and watched an old movie on Turner Classics, and ordered out from Three Bow Thai. She over-tipped the delivery boy. She had spring rolls, Tod Mun Pla with sweet duck sauce, and chicken satay on those thin wooden skewers. As usual, she got down one bite of each before her stomach rebelled.

At eleven, she got into bed.

This time, when the buzzer rang it was just after two a.m. She took her time getting ready. Over her pajamas she donned Bart's raincoat, the one with the deep pockets. In one she dropped the switchblade, in the other the mace. The air gun was easy to hide inside the folds.

"Motherfucking cunt!" Rudy announced as he careened past, stinking of sweat and booze. He had his keys out. He made it to his apartment door, but as he attempted to work the locks, he leaned against it and the door opened, surprising him. He fell forward. Arlene waited for the grunt, the groan, the inevitable string of expletives. But minutes passed.

Arlene saw Rudy's half-laced shoes, extending out past the doorframe. Like the wicked witch, she thought, but he wasn't exactly melting. Yet he could have hit his head in just the right way. He could be bleeding to death right now. She imagined turning and going upstairs. In the morning, she'd discover his prone body and phone the proper authorities. But what if he was only knocked unconscious, what if he came to in the night, and crawled into bed, what then? They'd be back to square one. Slowly, ever so slowly, she inched down the hall. Rudy lay prone, face down. There was a gap between the bottom of his pants and his socks, showing pallid, sickly flesh. Was he breathing? Arlene pushed at him, with her foot, tentatively. No response.

She tried again, harder.

Then her baby kicked. Arlene told herself, Rudy was a human being too, he was someone's son. He could be seriously hurt. Wasn't that what you wanted, she reminded herself, and that was when his legs snapped together round her ankles, and she tumbled backwards. Her back hit the banister, a brilliant, jabbing pain.

"Bitch," he hissed.

She managed to get her balance. But Rudy was up, pressing her back into the corner of the hallway, mashing her belly as he did. She tried to dig her hands into her pockets, but he had her trapped. As for the gun, it had slipped out of her grasp when he tripped her, dropping onto the floor with a clatter. "Let me go!" But it came out hoarse, blurred by fear. Then, "You're hurting the baby."

"Where's my money?" he demanded, not giving her an inch of breathing space. "You did get it, right?"

"Yes," she said.

"You got it upstairs?"

"Upstairs, yes."

"Good girl. I knew I could count on you." Rudy finally eased up. The gun was at their feet, but he didn't look down. Instead, he let her go, and turned his back. He'd made his point, she realized. He'd terrified her, he'd showed her exactly who was in charge.

"Why are you doing this to us?" she asked.

Rudy let out a guttural laugh. He turned, and eyed her contemptuously. "You mean you don't know yet?"

She shook her head.

"I'm doing it because I can," he said. Then he shut his apartment door.

Arlene waited for her heart to stop racing, then she reached down and picked up the air rifle. She thought how stupid she'd been, crazy, and also, that in a second he was going to come back out here, he was going to see his television set demolished and what then? She knew she had to get away from him, had to get back upstairs and turn both locks, and she had managed to take a few steps when she heard the creak of the floorboards directly above her head. Her breath caught. She listened, hard, tilting her right ear towards the ceiling. The unmistakable sound of someone walking away from the hallway, towards her living room.

Bart was home, she told herself and impulsively started towards him, then knew better, Bart was in Italy, he'd called her from there only hours ago, this wasn't her husband arriving home to save her. This was trouble. The 911 variety. Rudy had the closest phone. But it was smarter to go next door, to the neighbors. She started towards the front door, and then heard the squeak of the staircase. He, whoever he was, was heading down.

Arlene opened Rudy's door, and shut it softly behind her. She lifted the phone, but there was no dial tone. They cut the wires, she thought, then flashed on that pile of unpaid bills. She heard voices, right outside the door. She heard a male voice say, "Shit!"

The back door in the kitchen led to the garden, but there were locks on it, and a key for the iron safety door outside. She had no idea where Rudy kept it.

Trapped, she thought and saw herself, on her knees, pleading, asking them to spare the baby.

There was only the bedroom. Only Rudy to turn to for help.

Because she knew that she wasn't going to be able to lift the air gun and shoot them, and even if she did, they could be better armed.

Shaking him, she got a "Wha?"

"Rudy, someone's broken in," she said. Then, before she could check it, "help me, please!"

His eyelids fluttered, then relaxed.

Turning, she heard the door creak open.

"Would you look at that. Open Sesame," a voice said.

Arlene saw shadows falling on the living room floor, and she looked round desperately. The closet? But she didn't even have time for that. She dropped down behind the bed and turned on her side, wedging herself underneath.

"My man Rudy."

Arlene saw white Nike high tops, with red stripes darting round the toe.

"Rudy, you better wake the fuck up."

Then the bed creaked. And she heard the sound of an open handed slap.

"What the fuck you think … !" From Rudy.

Another slap, or maybe a punch, the bed shook.

"Where's the goddamn money?"

"Whaddyamean?"

"What do I mean? What do you mean, telling us some goddamn story. You think we've got time to waste on you? There's no fucking money to be had. No twenty G's."

"You're crazy. She told me she got it." Then a crafty edge to his voice, he added, "Who you bluffing now? You're trying to keep it for yourself?"

"I surely am not."

"Well then go back, beat up the bitch, and look again."

"What bitch? There's no one up there. Not a soul."

"Where'd she go, she was just here?"

"Was she? Well she vacated the damn premises."

"She said it was up there, they've got plenty of shit up there."

"Nothing I need. You promised us each three grand if we scored this. Right, Dino?"

"Right as rain," the other voice said.

"You with your big talk, how it was gonna be easy, how she would just hand it over and we'd be home free, how you had her scared and on the run. On the run all right, she ran off. Or maybe she wasn't there at all. Maybe it's just you, Rudy, trying to get over on me again."

"I wasn't doing nothing like that."

"How's a man to tell with you?"

"Yeah," the other voice said. "How's a man to tell."

"You know what Rudy? The way I see it, you've been fucking with me. And I don't like that. I think you're pretty much of a useless excuse for a human being."

"There's no reason to say that to me," Rudy told him. The bed squeaked, and then she saw Rudy's feet on the floor.

"So, where's our money?"

"I told you, she's got it stashed up there."

"As in, you're not paying. I ought to break your arms for you," he said. "Dino here, he ought to do your fingers first, one at a time. We ought to do something nice and old school to make you suffer."

"Guys, come on, you just didn't look in the right spot."

"You're gonna show us the right spot? You know something I don't all of a sudden?"

"Maybe I do," Rudy said.

"You know what I think," he said. "I think this is the last fucking goose chase I'm going on for you. I'm sick of your bullshit, man!"

"Hey," Rudy said, "Manny, there's no call to … " There were two quick pops. Little soft sounds. And then Rudy was there, next to her on the ground, staring right at her, blood coursing down from the top of his head. He twitched, then went limp. She shoved her hand into her mouth, because a scream came next. Arlene shut her eyes.

She heard them walking away, "Look at this, someone fucked with his TV."

"Maybe he did it himself."

Then the door of the apartment shut.

When she was sure they were gone, she pulled herself out, and stood up. She didn't look at Rudy. Upstairs, she saw they'd made quite a mess. Lifting the phone, she stuck in those three magic numbers. "Please state your name and the type of emergency," the operator said. Arlene imagined what the police would say, what they would do, how she might be called on to testify if she told the whole truth. She set the phone back down, telling herself it was better to wait until morning and discover him like that. Better for everyone concerned.

But now, if she did some smart detective might look up her phone records, and see that another call had been placed, earlier. Then they'd take her into the backroom of the station and pepper her with questions. *So you went shopping for a gun yourself, you were afraid of this man, weren't you?* What to do? Arlene thought about phoning Bart, but that was even more ridiculous.

It seemed easy when you watched people doing it in the movies, or on TV, but it was hard work rolling Rudy onto the Hudson Bay blanket, Bart's favorite. She wrapped up Rudy's body and bound him. Pushed him, shoved him, rolled and cajoled to get him into the hallway, then all the way to the front door.

Their Mercedes wagon was parked in a lot two blocks away. She went and got it and double parked in front of the house. The sky was getting lighter, and Arlene realized she had very little time to get this done.

And then she felt a wrenching pain. She could hardly breathe. There was no mistaking that pain.

She bent to her task with a burst of outsized energy, dragging him across the threshold, down the steps, his head bouncing off each one and onto the pavement, the body curled up in its shroud, and then, shoving and pushing and pulling and stopping every few minutes to let the searing pain subside. When the burning subsided, she did it again, until finally she had him stretched across the backseat, his body stiffening slightly so that she had to close the door, then bang it shut, trying not to think of what bones she was breaking on him in the process.

The park was basically a strip of ground that overlooked the East River. They'd come here a few times, eating lunch together on the weekends. To her left was the Manhattan Bridge, to her right, the Williamsburg. She knew that the river current was thick and violent. She parked right at the top of the hill that led straight down to the water.

Even though the embankment was steep she had to follow him down, making her way slowly across the slick grass and rocks. Arlene kicked at Rudy, pounded at him, and finally he set off, tumbling into the water. He bobbed and weaved, and then sank. Arlene went back to the car, got her air gun and the other fine, useless implements of destruction. They made three gentle splashes. Lifting her eyes she saw the southernmost tip of Manhattan and then realized that the Eastern sky was turning violet, the sun was about to come up.

At Brooklyn Methodist, Arlene told the admitting nurse she was having a baby.

In two hours more, she did, a girl.

"Do you have a name?" the nurse asked. Arlene didn't even pause for a second. "Katherine," she said. It was her baby. It was damn well going to be her choice.

POETRY
EXISTENTIALISM
AND BOCCE

WAITING FOR GALLO
CHARLIE STELLA

Nicky Lombardo picked up Joey Rizzo in a stolen Honda Accord outside the Canarsie train station. He drove the length of Rockaway Parkway to the traffic circle at the pier, turned into the parking lot, and found a spot two rows from Abbracciamento's. It was a few minutes past midnight when Lombardo turned the engine off. The restaurant had stopped serving food at eleven. The bar would close at one. The man they were waiting for would be out within the hour.

"Who's he in there with?" Rizzo asked.

"The smoke he's banging," Lombardo said. "The one the fuss is all about."

Rizzo fidgeted with the Walther P1 he found under the seat. He leaned forward to heft the handgun under the dashboard before Lombardo nudged him with an elbow. Rizzo looked up and saw a young black couple walking along the pier. He set the gun on the floor between his feet.

"It's hard to get used to, huh?" Lombardo said. "The way this place has changed."

"You're not kidding," Rizzo said. "I took the train in from the city, I'm looking around, feels like I'm in a movie. Fuckin' *Twilight Zone*, the graffiti all over. Then this tonight, Charlie Gallo? We go back thirty-five years."

Lombardo was still watching the couple. He pointed at them when they kissed. "When did all this happen?"

"Whenever the first one bought a house," Rizzo said. "I know my old man sold soon's he heard one of them bought across from Holy Family. Then it was like dominoes, one family after another. It's our own fault. We're the ones ran."

Lombardo turned away from the black couple. "Was like cancer the way it spread. Flatlands down to Seaview, down the park there, even the Paerdegats, once they put that high school up, South Shore. Then the floodgates opened. Even Mill Basin now, over by Ralph Avenue, that's all shines now too."

"Used to be Jew and Italian, Canarsie."

"The only blacks back then lived in the projects," said Lombardo, thumbing over his left shoulder. "Seaview back there and Brookline back across Flatlands. Now the only white guys around here are Russians, and those fuckin' people don't care where they live."

Rizzo took a moment to glance around the pier. "Least they fixed this place up," he said. "It never looked this good when we were kids."

Both men had grown up on opposite ends of Canarsie more than thirty years ago. Lombardo had moved out to Long Island during his freshman year in high school. Rizzo's family had waited until after he graduated.

"Still spic city, the pier," Lombardo said. "Every weekend is the Puerto Rican Day parade over here."

Two restaurant workers wearing white uniforms pulled large plastic garbage bags out a door behind the restaurant. They stacked the bags inside a metal container before stopping to smoke.

Rizzo said, "How the fuck this happen with Charlie? He ran a little shy and a small sheet. What's this got to do with a broad?"

"She's somebody's wife."

"Not a made guy, she's black."

"Somebody as in a detective on Tommy Agro's payroll. Guy did his own snooping, caught his wife and your friend Charlie in the sack. Got pictures he says he can't live with anymore, what Agro said."

Rizzo made a face. "Pictures? Tell him throw her out and get a divorce. He can burn the fuckin' pictures."

"It was up to me, yeah, you're right, but this is Agro's call. The cop is with organized crime. Charlie's just another nobody."

"Where'd he meet her? Charlie moved out to Bay Ridge five, six years ago."

"Dentist office, according to Agro. She's a hygienist there in his neighborhood."

Rizzo shook his head in disgust. "We lived around the corner from each other," he said. "Charlie was on Ninety-fifth between L and M. We lived on Ninety-sixth. I know him since I'm ten. The old Canarsie trolley used to run between our blocks before our time. Behind our yards was a drop to where the tracks used to be. We used to play war in there. Baseball when we got older. One of the old timers had a garden, he grew vegetables, had fig trees, grape vines, the whole thing. We used his barricade around the garden as a home run fence. It was like fantasy land. We made the place whatever we wanted it to be."

"And now it's a ghetto," Lombardo said.

Rizzo didn't hear him. He said, "Even here, the pier. We used to come here to crab. They had that boat ride, remember? Was next to the bait house. It was a big deal to go on that boat we were kids. My mother used to take us on the bus, the forty-two. Charlie too, he used to come along."

Lombardo shrugged. "Now he's dating shines."

"Huh?"

"Your friend, now he's chasing spades."

Rizzo squinted. "What's your point?"

"I'm just saying, one minute he's playing games with you in the back yard there, thirty years ago, crabbing on the pier here, and now he's going down on brillo pad trim's gonna cost him his life."

"Brillo pad? What's the difference she's black? He's getting a piece is all. Don't tell me it bothers you she's black."

"Hey, it's got nothin' to do with me, Joe, okay? Charlie likes dark meat, more power to 'em, but this is Agro's call. The cop, he's more important than Charlie, end of story."

Rizzo shook his head again. "The guy was in my wedding party for Christ sakes. He had my back I don't know how many times when we were growing up. He took a beating with me over in Neponsit, the beach there, he could've just as easy kept driving, made believe he didn't see us. Half a dozen scumbags from Rosedale jumped me and Louie C. on our way back from the beach. Charlie saw it and pulled over to help us. Got stitches in his head for stopping."

Lombardo said, "Look, Agro has an arrangement with this coon detective. Charlie's nailing the guy's wife, it don't make a difference he's a friend, he got stitches thirty years ago."

"It's not right," Rizzo said. "I wouldn't mind they give him a warning. Break his teeth, you wanna make a point. His legs, you gotta, but a guy's entitled to chase a piece. Since when he's gotta pay for it like this, he hits on the wrong broad?"

"You're trying to make sense of something you can't. It's got nothing to do with Charlie or his chasing trim. It's about the cop. He's got a hook into an O.C. unit. That's all Agro cares about. You can't blame him, you think about it. He's probably what keeps Agro on the street, this cop."

Rizzo wasn't listening. He was seeing his friend from thirty-five years ago. He said, "Charlie used to help old man Catalano out after his stroke. Used to take care of things, water the plants, take out the garbage, whatnot. We were like twelve, thirteen. Used to make me feel guilty for not waking up in time to help."

Lombardo chuckled. "You wanna tell that to Tommy Agro, he used to water the plants, take out the garbage, see if it gets your friend a pass?"

"I'm just saying. I know his daughter, for Christ sakes. I see her a couple times a year. She married my son's best friend. They come over the house around the holidays. New Year's, Easter, like that. She used to be friends with my daughter."

Lombardo took one last drag from his cigarette before tossing it out the window.

Rizzo said, "Maybe you shouldn't have told me."

"And then what? You walk up to pop a guy and have to stop because he's your friend?"

"They fuckin' send me for anyway? I like the motherfucker."

"That's exactly why," Lombardo told him. "And you know it. Because you like the guy, he likes you. You can get close in case he's around people you know."

Rizzo pulled a pack of Camel cigarettes from his jacket pocket. "Who the fuck do I know around here anymore?"

Lombardo pushed the dashboard lighter in. "Still without the filters?"

Rizzo held his left hand over the lighter waiting for it to pop out. "Couldn't this cop straighten this broad out on his own?"

"Apparently not."

"The cocksucker."

"She's a looker too. Supposed to be. Something like fifteen years younger than the husband."

Rizzo lit his cigarette. "Asshole couldn't find something his own age?"

"Agro claims she's for show, the wife. The cop likes white meat."

"It's fucked up."

"I says to Tommy, 'Don't they all?'"

"Don't they all what?"

"Like white meat."

"Oh. What Agro say?"

"It's none of my fuckin' business."

Rizzo took a drag on his cigarette.

"I seen the cop in Tommy's club on McDonald Avenue," Lombardo said. "Cost him fifty bucks before he got one of the skanks down the basement there. He wanted Shelly, the blonde works the bar, but she said she'd kill herself first."

Rizzo was clearly annoyed at the story. He said, "Yeah? So, how come we're not whacking her?"

Lombardo said, "Look, Joe, this is too important to go into with hesitation. Agro give it to me, I gotta get it done. We handle this, when the books open, we're both sitting pretty."

Rizzo forced a chuckle. "The books," he said, "another fuckin' joke. They open for special cases like that mutt, punk, fuckfaced scumbag from Staten Island, Jackie Fina. And how long it take him to flip, about five minutes? For some bullshit assault with a baseball bat would've netted him all of two years. Jackie-boy was giving away names before they finished cuffing him."

"Which is why guys like you and me are still waiting. Jack Fina had bloodlines working for him. His old man and his uncle. Both were standup."

"Yeah, so? Jack is a fuckin' rat."

"He was a piece of shit, yeah, but they straightened him out young because he had clout going in. They won't be giving it away like that again anytime soon, don't worry. It's back to the old ways ever since that fiasco. But this thing tonight is a huge step in the right direction. We both got work under our belts, but this is special."

"This is bullshit," Rizzo said. "Whacking one of our own for some cop can't control his wife. The fuck's it coming to?"

"What's it coming to? What's it always been? It is what it is."

"It's a fuckin' joke is what it is."

"Yeah, well, forget this work tonight, how it bothers you, whatever. You don't wanna repeat that in fronna' the wrong set of ears, you think it's a joke."

Rizzo waved it off. "I'm just saying is all. We used to go the movies together, me and this guy. We saw *The Longest Day* at the theatre there on Avenue L, I don't know how many times one weekend. The lunches at Joe's Pizza on the L back when you couldn't eat meat Fridays. Then, during the week, we had a few bucks, we'd go to Grabstein's on Rockaway Parkway, get a pastrami, a knish. We used to do everything together, Charlie and me. Here he is a piece of work now. And for what, some cop?"

"We had cops on the payroll before and the bosses back then did the same thing Agro's doing now. You keep them happy, do them favors, whatever the fuck it takes, because a cop in that position can keep your ass out the shit."

"Guy goes through life, the ups and downs, gets married, has a couple kids, winds up divorced, he still gets up every day, takes care of business," Rizzo said. "That's Charlie. That's his story. Nothing flashy, but he takes care of business. Now he meets some broad, he gets along, he don't, who the fuck knows? I don't. Maybe they're good for each other. Maybe they're in love. Fuck's the difference. She's with him tonight, her husband's wherever the fuck he is, out of town no doubt, we're doing this, what, he deserves to die? Bullshit."

Lombardo was looking at his watch. He glanced up at the restaurant and let out a breath of frustration.

Rizzo said, "Sorry I'm boring you, Nicky, okay? I'll shut the fuck up you want."

"What I want is to get this thing over with," Lombardo said. "Frankly, I'm worried you can get it done, you like the guy so much."

"Don't worry about me," Rizzo said. "I'll do the work. I'll shoot Charlie Gallo in the fuckin' head like he's a piece of shit, which he isn't. You'll look good for Agro, don't worry."

Lombardo took offense. "Yeah, and so will you look good too," he said.

Both men stared at each other until Rizzo nodded. "Fair enough," he said.

A small group of people appeared around one corner of the restaurant. Lombardo craned his neck to see.

"The fuck is he?"

Rizzo looked up and saw the man they were waiting for walking with a tall black woman. "There," he said, pointing at them.

Lombardo started the engine. "Get your stuff," he said.

Rizzo was already pulling on a pair of dark gloves. He removed a black skull mask from under the seat and stretched it out to fit on top of his head. He picked the Walther off the floor and racked the slide.

"Ready?" Lombardo asked.

Rizzo glanced up at the couple walking across the lot. The man stopped alongside the passenger door of a white Ford Taurus. He opened the door for the woman.

"Joe?" Lombardo said.

"Go," Rizzo said.

Lombardo drove across the lot as the man walked around the back of the Taurus. Twenty yards away, Lombardo turned on the headlights. The man turned toward the Honda. Lombardo turned on the high beams and the man shielded his eyes from the glare.

Rizzo had pulled down the mask to cover his face. He was out of the car as soon as it stopped. His friend of more than thirty-five years raised both hands when he saw the gun. Rizzo shot him twice in the chest before standing over the body and shooting another two bullets into Charlie Gallo's head. He could hear the woman screaming inside the Taurus. He glared at her through the window before getting back inside the Honda.

Five minutes later, Lombardo turned onto the exit for Cross Bay Boulevard. Rizzo had removed the mask and was wiping down the Walther. He kept the gloves on as he wrapped the gun with black electric tape. When it was fully covered, he set the gun on the floor.

"I don't know you wanna hear it or not, but good job," Lombardo said.

"Thanks," Rizzo said. "And no hard feelings before. It's just I knew the guy."

Lombardo slapped Rizzo on the leg. "Forgetaboutit," he said, running the words together.

"And you were right about the woman," Rizzo said. "She is a looker."

Lombardo smiled. "Well, at least he had that then, your friend. At least he had that."

"Yeah," Rizzo said. "I guess."

STONES
KEN BRUEN

MY OLD MAN WAS A COP, NOT a very good one but he bought it in the line of duty, so I guess, that makes him … what, a hero? … or an asshole?

He'd be seriously disappointed in me … he was second generation Irish and as Celtic as the shamrock, my mother was Park Slope and when she bought the farm, I got the house. It's a piece if shit but hey, what can I tell you, it's a place, if not a home. My old man, he used to read poetry, how fucked is that? The guy wears the blue, gets to carry a piece and legit, and what, he comes home, every evening, has shot of Jameson and starts to read fucking poems? Me, I don't read. The sports page, maybe, get me the Daily News, see how the Jets are choking.

Like that

But I got me some serious damage going. And if I'm not like, real careful, I'll be buying the farm.

A woman of course……what else and gotta say, a looker, else, why the hassle. Me and John, cruising along Livonia Avenue a few weeks back and we see this nigger giving it large to a woman. Hitting her repeatedly in the face, right there on the corner. I say to John

"Whoa, hold the phones."

He glances over, his long black hair obscuring his face, mutters

"Nigger shit."

But he pulls the Buick over, fucking gas guzzler but that's John, Brooklyn, the Mets and America, did a stint in the first Desert Storm and truth to tell, he's been kinda weird ever since. What the hell, I can do weird, been doing it all me goddamned life and what, he's my buddy, my main guy, walked point for me more times than I can remember so I put up with his shit. He goes

"Charlie, let it go bro."

As if......

I get out of the car, the tire iron in me left hand, the way we do it in Brooklyn, nothing showy but with intent. Call

"Hey, dude, what's shaking."

The nigger is built, like a shithouse and mean with it, he stops punching the woman, gives a lazy smile, those mothers, on meth or some crap, asks

"I know you homes?"

I smile too, say

"Don't call me homes."

Take him from the chin up with the iron, the Canarsie special we call it, puts your teeth right up behind your eyes and to keep it light, we add

"Lemme rock your world."

Rocked his

Flat on his back, blood seeping from his mouth, he's all done. I look at the woman, a beaut, I mean, your heart stopper, red hair, fresh open face, with lips to die for. The way things been going, I might have to, I go

"You okay?"

and her bruised face, beautiful it was, lights up and she goes

"Am now."

To cut to the chase, she comes along in the Buick, I go

"John, this is Rose."

He grunts.

What's he going to do, argue with me?

Her name wasn't Rose but I kind of thought she looked like a crushed flower so Rose it was.

Later, we had a few brews in a place in Brooklyn that's still authentic, i.e..........affordable. The other side of Jack and Bud's, John takes off and Rose and me, well, we end up back at my house, get it on in the front room

The lounge, as my mother called it, I had a bottle of Bushmills, left over from me old man's stock and we have a few belts of that. I was in the bag, else why I'd do what I next did?

Got me old man's book of poetry down, read her the one poem, "Stones," that he was always on about.

The first time he read it for me, I sneered

"The guy's from Brooklyn, no way, we don't do poetry."

He slaps me the upside of me head, I told you he was a cop, it's what they do and goes

"You ignorant pup, he's not only a poet, he drives an oil truck, don't see you riding anything but your poor mother. Busting her chops from morning till night."

I tried to imitate his rich voice, that lilt them Micks have, like music without melody, go

I was seventeen
 Before I knew
My eyes were blue
That girls liked them
That girls liked my eyes
That they were blue
Until then
I was too busy
Throwing stones
Throwing stones at the mirror

And never got to finish, she was on her knees, giving me the blow job of me life

Poetry.......and to think I used to say, it sucked

What's the current buzz? Oh yeah, we became an item. John was pissed, went

"The fuck you at bro?"

I gave him the look, asked

"Why are you talking like a nig?"

His face creased in that frown he'd get when he was really losing it, he said

"We have some nice scams going, we're doing okay, and you want to run around with a woman who's, like, serious trouble?"

John was doing the driving, he'd turned off Belt Parkway onto Bay Seventeenth Street. I noticed a nice white clapboard house to my left. He followed my eyes, said

"You're thinking you and *Rose might* settle in someplace like that?"

His voice was spit, he used her name like a bad taste in his mouth. Time to take him off the board, I turned from the house, gave him my granite look, asked

"What's with you buddy, you don't even know her, why such a hard on for her?"

He was trying to avoid a gypsy cab that was meandering all over the road, probably the driver was Lithuanian, he certainly wasn't from Brooklyn. John said

"I know her, that black guy, she'd been with him for a year, yeah, the love of your life was giving it up to a spade and he's a dealer, got some heavy crew running with him and you………you slap him on the upside of his head and then shack up with his woman…….. the fuck is the matter with you?"

I'd been wondering how to broach the deal and here was the chance, said

"Kareem, that's his name, he's into moving freight all right and Rose say's he's ripe for the taking."

John thumped the wheel, going

"I knew it, you stoopid motherfucker."

It was a simple plan, aren't they all?

Come the first Friday of the month, like the Catholic church, Kareem took stock, got all his cash together, had all the runners give it up and then bring it to a bank in Manhattan

The fuck, he's earning all this in Brooklyn? And wont even let the local banks get it. Reason enough to take him off, like, for the community. Ever since the Dodgers were stolen from us and yeah,

I mean *stolen*, every bastard and his mother think they can rip us off. Not any more, not if I could help it.

Using my most patient tone, I laid out all this for John, get him fired up, get him on board. He might be crazy but he's one of our own. He had the radio on, he always needed noise, I guess after The Gulf, silence was its own punishment

The song playing then, I don't buy into omens, superstitions, all that *shite*, as my old man called it but maybe I should have taken heed, it was Morrissey with *First of the gang to die.*

John looked at me, said

"Are you jerking my chain, when'd you get so riled up about The Dodgers, you're a goddamn Jets fan."

A sore point, especially as they'd just had their ass handed to them

We were cruising near Belt Parkway, coming up on Ocean Parkway, man, that is a mess, all those ramps, overpasses, exits. What's with that ?

I got my accent in gear, went

"I'm a Brooklyn guy, huh, you see me moving out, you see me moving into Man-hatt-an?"

He was agitated, his hair swinging and licking his teeth, a tic that spelled trouble, he said

"You're moving all right, slam dunk into a mess of grief."

But he agreed, took a time, I'll give him that but it was never on the cards that he'd bail, he was my buddy, what choice did he have?

So he bitched and tried to talk me out of it but he was in. I let him handle the hardware, he was a grunt, he knew that shit. And more important, he knew some boyos who operated out of Norstrand Avenue. I'd gone over there once with him, the apartment decorated with Crosses from Long Kesh or as they called it…. *The Kesh*, Harps on the walls and lots of cans of Guinness and of course, bottles of Jameson. They respected John as he'd seen action and me, they tolerated as I was second generation Mick but they weren't too hot on my attitude. This rat faced runt offers me a Jameson and I go

"Got any Calvert?"

He looks at John, *who is this guy?* And asks

"The fook is that?"

After we got out of there, John said

"No offense Charlie, they don't want you coming round no more."

Gee, like that hurt?

I said

"You mean I wont get to hear about *The Cause* no more"

He got a sawn off and a Glock, I go

"You're a little short there buddy."

He thought I meant the sawn off, said

"Close work, you don't need no long barrel"

I laughed, he really was one dumb son of a bitch, I said

"Two weapons, what about Rose?"

He was as close to a spit as I'd ever seen him, said

"Women and guns, no way bro."

Before I could attack, he said

"Besides, we need someone to drive the car, seeing as we're gonna be heavy with cash."

Like he believed it for a New York minute.

I let it slide, don't sweat the small stuff. I didn't know that Rose was already prepared and I don't just mean the small caliber she carried in her purse. Lock n load, oh, she had that gig covered.

My Dad, with his thick cop face, his Irish coloring, part bar tan and part graveyard pale loved to utter proclamations, when he wasn't doing the 1916 Declaration of Independence, and I wanted to roar ... *You're a goddamn American, do the The Patriot one,* he was stating

"There's them who can read the writing on the wall and then there's them who put it there."

Deep huh?

He'd always pause at this point, to have a wee sip of Jameson, for dramatic effect, then, he'd add the rider, the kicker

"You me boy, are neither."

Thing is, now I know, he had a point

Else how do you explain my complete refusal to face the fact of Rose. I got to see her in action and shrugged it off. I could say I was in love but John would say, I was in heat.

There used to be a bar on Cumberland Street, owned by an Italian guy, I dunno was he connected but he was certainly motivated, ran the place like a Starbucks on speed, doing all the serving his own self. The three of us had a table near the back drinking Bud and Jack chasers. I'd knocked off a minor credit card scam and we were celebrating. John took off early, saying he'd a hot date

Yeah, right.

Like any woman would look at him, twice. I was a little pissed that he took the cash but couldn't like, what give me an hour to savour the scam, the fuck is with that? I went

What-the-fuck-ever …

Fuming

Next minute, my head would have been tilted and my finger pointing, the prelude to violence. Rose was rubbing my thigh, passed me a joint, said

"Chill baby, go to the restroom, have a joke."

I did

I brought the rage down a notch, came out of the restroom and some skel is hanging over the table, leering at Rose, I think

"Uh oh, here we go, rock n fucking roll."

Before I even get there, she's smashed her glass against the rim of the table and gouged it into the guy's face, screaming

"You cocksucker."

There's one of those slow motion moments, everything is still, then chaos rules supreme. The guy is wailing like a banshee, buckets of blood streaming from his ruined face, Rose is on her feet, trying to kick him in the head and the Italian owner is over the counter, baseball bat in hand

For whom?

Rose?

I drop him real fast and we're out of there, running up the street, cries behind us and I realize she's ... *laughing*

We get back to my place and she's all over me, like some cat, tearing me clothes off, and we go at it like primitives, she lets her head back, mid orgasm, shrieks ... Stones

So what I'd learn from that little episode

Not to fuck with her

John is round early the next morning, going

"The fuck happened?"

I'm stretching, hangover kicking in, had me some Jameson after the wrestling and maybe overdid it. I go

"No biggie."

He's shaking his head, says

"She takes a guy out, you got the guineas looking for you and you don't ever want those guys doing that and you're what, stretching?"

I told him it was all smoke, not to sweat it and he get's right in my face, says

"Charlie, she's got to go, she's medieval."

I needed some coffee, a lot of coffee and some aspirin, shrug him off with

"The girl has some cojones on her, you fault her for that, you might take a lesson from her, stop whining all the goddamn time."

He slammed the door on the way out

Hard

Rose, later,

"Your buddy, John Boy, he doesn't like me."

I'm trying to roll a joint, she got me into the habit of weed in the morning, brings the dimmer down real low and I said

"He'll come round, nothing to worry about."

She had her hand on my crotch, purred
"He's gay, that it?"
Jesus

Taking down the drug dealer, Kareem went like a piece of cake, we were in and out in jig time, leaving Kareem with a face full of sawn off. Back at the house, I was mid count, mid snort of the fine coke when Rose shot John in the back of the head, muttering
"Faggot."
She put two in my gut and they're right, that is the worst agony, she leaned over me, whispered
"You know what, I fucking hate poetry, it's not a Brooklyn thing."

BOCCE BALL

KING of FARRAGUT ROAD

ROBERT RANDISI

THE BOCCE BALL KING OF FARRAGUT ROAD
Robert J. Randisi

THIS ISN'T REALLY ABOUT ME.

Well, okay, it is, sort of, but it has more to do with the man I knew as old Mr. DiCicca when I was a kid.

I guess I should explain that I'm talkin' about back in the '50s, when my Puerto Rican Grandfather—who we all called "Poppy"—lived on East Ninety-fifth Street in Brooklyn, between Foster Avenue and Farragut Road in Canarsie. See, my mother was Puerto Rican and my father was Italian. Two cultures that are not so different and have a history. They came to this country at just about the same time, although on different boats, you might say. Both my parents grew up in Manhattan but eventually my whole family—grandparents included, except for my paternal grandfather, who walked out when my father was young—ended up in Brooklyn. Poppy and Grandma Velez bought a big house on East Ninety-fifth Street which, at odd times, had some of us kids living in the front portion while they inhabited the back and rented out the upstairs. My grandfather owned quite a few properties in Canarsie and pretty much lived off the rents, but that's another story.

My sister and I lived there for a while until our parents bought a house of their own in a newly developed section of Canarsie. All the homes on that block were huge, many with second floors and a wrap-around porch. In present day many of them have either been torn down or rehabbed and sold for a fortune. There were hardly any brick houses at all on that block when I was growing up, then one day they cleared some land and built all these two-story, two-family attached brick homes. That's when the block began to change.

But enough of my family history. All you need to know is that my grandfather owned a house in what was predominantly an Italian neighborhood at the time. Right next to the house was an alleyway which actually ran for blocks, but next to Poppy's house the old Italian men had constructed a bocce ball court. The Italian neighbors were very friendly with Poppy, even though he didn't play bocce with them.

But it was my father who used to go out there and compete from time and to time, and I'd watch. (He also played poker with them on Friday nights.) I remember being five years old, watching Dad and the old Italian men rolling those wooden balls down the court. I didn't know all the rules—still don't—but it had something to do with getting your balls closer to another ball in order to score points.

I always wondered why Dad—who must have been thirty at the time, no more—bothered to associate with the old men. See, that's all they were to me at the time, old Italian men who usually smelled of garlic and had sauce stains on their shirts and trousers. Oh, don't get me wrong, they dressed well enough, with a crease in their pants and the top button done on their shirts but they cooked a lot, ate even more, and usually had some sort of stain somewhere, almost like a badge of courage—or cooking.

And the oldest of all seemed to be old Mr. DiCicca. But as old as he was—or seemed to me—he was respected, almost revered by the others, and he was referred to as the Bocce Ball King of Farragut Road because he usually won. (I know, the alley and the court were on East Ninety-fifth Street, but I guess the name sounded better than Bocce Ball King of East Ninety-fifth Street.)

The day I want to talk about, though, is the day I found out that Mr. DiCicca was more than just a Bocce Ball King.

Back in those days before air conditioning it used to get really hot at night, and when I couldn't sleep I'd sneak outside to try to get some air. Sometimes there would be kids—teenagers—in the alley—boys and girls—necking and doing stuff that boys and girls did. Poppy had planted bushes all around the house, just inside a chain link fence, so we'd have some privacy when we were in the yard. I had carved out a space for myself beneath a set of those bushes where I could lie on my stomach and watch. Sometimes, during the day, I'd watch the bocce ball matches from there, but at night I'd watch other things.

On this night, I watched something I would never forget, something that forever changed my opinion of old Mr. DiCicca.

After sneaking out of the house I thought I heard voices in the alley. I went to my niche beneath the bushes, slipped myself comfortably into it, and stared out through the chain links at a group of men who had gathered on the bocce ball court. There was enough moonlight to see the faces of the men who were not shrouded in shadows, or turned away from me. The one I recognized right away was Mr. DiCicca. He was dressed much the way he would dress for a bocce ball match. Aside from him there were four other men. The only other face I could see clearly was the man who was on his knees, a look of sheer terror on his face. I didn't know what was going on, but I was entranced.

"Please, my Don," the kneeling man said in English, "I—I didn't know she was your granddaughter."

"You dishonor me an-a my family," Mr. DiCicca said, "an-a your excuse is-a that you didn't know?"

"Please, Don—"

"Silence!"

I'd never heard the old man speak with such power and force before. Also, I didn't know at the time why the kneeling man was calling him "Don."

"Vito," DiCicca said to one of his men, "the Pallino."

"I knew from watching my father play with them that the "Pallino" was the small, target ball that everyone tried to get their bocce balls near to score points. I wondered what kind of bocce ball game this was.

The man called Vito stepped forward and handed DiCicca the small ball. I can't recall now if the faces of the other three men were constantly shadowed, or if I was just remembering it that way. I didn't even know if they were Mr. DiCicca's age, or the other man's. However, the faces of Mr. DiCicca and the kneeling man were forever etched into my mind that night.

"Open-a you' mouth, Nicky," DiCicca said to the kneeling man.

"Wha—I—"

"Open it!"

The kneeling man, Nicky, opened his mouth wide, but not wide enough to suit DiCicca.

"Help him!" he said to the others, in disgust.

The other three men stepped forward. Two of them grabbed an arm each and the third man held Nicky's jaw in his hand, digging his fingers in so that the kneeling man had no choice but to open his mouth.

DiCicca approached him, holding in his hand the Pallino. From what I could see then—and, of course, what I learned later—it was roughly the size of a cue ball. The little old man I knew was growing in stature before my eyes with each passing second.

"You never play bocce ball with us Nicky," he said. "Why is-a that? Is it because it is not a young-a man's game? Eh? The same reason you don't a-speak Italian? Because-a you young and you have-a no respect?"

Nicky tried to answer, but the third man would not allow him to close his mouth enough to form words.

"Well," DiCicca said, "today we are going to a-play a different form of bocce ball, eh?"

With that DiCicca reached out and pressed the Pallino to the man's mouth. At first it didn't fit, but the old man placed his other hand behind Nicky's head and then pushed the ball until it popped into the kneeling man's mouth with an audible click as it broke some teeth. Nicky screamed. The man holding his jaw stepped away, because he was no longer needed to hold Nicky's mouth open. The Pallino was doing that. The other two men maintained their hold on his arms.

DiCicca stepped back to observe his handiwork, his face clearly illuminated by the moonlight. His skin looked dry, like sandpaper, and the way he was smiling I thought it would crack.

"Vito," he said to the third man, who had released Nicky's mouth.

"Yes, my Don?"

"Give-a me my red balls."

I had noticed while watching the men play bocce that Mr. DiCicca always rolled the red balls. Now Vito stepped forward and handed the older man two red balls.

"Hold-a him so his-a head leans a-forward," he told the other two men.

They obeyed, leaning the man over so his head almost hung. Nicky was still screaming when DiCicca stepped forward, held his hands wide with a ball in each, and then brought them together violently, catching Nicky's head between them. Apparently not satisfied, the old man did it again, and then again. I heard the dull sound, like the time my grandfather had dropped a melon and it had split when it hit the floor.

DiCicca was breathing hard and Vito hurried to him to take the balls from his hand.

The other two men released Nicky, who fell face forward onto the court. I could see blood from where his head had split and I must have gasped out loud.

"Who's that?" somebody said.

I was afraid to move. I thought if they found me they'd kill me, like they did the kneeling man. I remained as still as I could, and as quiet, and suddenly one of them leaned over and stared right at me through the chain links of the fence.

"It's a kid," he said.

He was staring right at me, although I didn't know if he could see my face, which must have been shadowed by the bushes. Galvanized into action I slid from my hiding place, unsure of where to run.

"It must be Joe Ravisi's boy," I heard Vito said. "Want me to get him?"

"No," the old man said, "leave-a him be. I am a-tired, Vito. We go home."

"But Don—"

"We go home!"

I didn't wait to see if they went home or not, or what they did with the body. I ran to the house, sneaked back inside, and hurried to my bed. I didn't bother to brush the dirt and twigs from my pajamas. Getting yelled at by my mother for dirtying my bed was the least of my worries.

2

The police came the next day.

It was dinner time, so we were all home, including my Dad. In fact, that night we were eating dinner with Poppy and Grandma, so we were all together around the table with the doorbell rang. My Dad got up and answered the door, came back to the dining room with a uniformed cop and a detective about my Dad's age who said his name was O'Connor. Turns out they knew each other because they went to the same bar.

"What's going on, Joe?" my mother asked.

"Terry, here, just wants to ask a few questions about the body they found in the alley this morning."

When we woke up that morning the police and an ambulance were in the alley. Pretty soon the word got passed through the neighborhood that a guy had been killed, probably by the Mafia. Although nobody actually said, "Mafia." Not in that neighborhood.

"That was horrible," she said. "Why would he want to question us?"

My father walked around behind my mother and put his hands on her shoulders.

"It's all right," he told her. "He's just doing his job. Go ahead, Terry."

"Well," the detective said, "we pretty much just want to know what, if anything, any of you heard last might, since this house is the closest to the, uh, murder?"

"Well," my Dad said, "I didn't hear a thing."

"Neither did I," my mother said.

My mother had to translate to Spanish for my grandmother, who said she hadn't heard a thing. That was most likely because several years before my grandmother had decided she was finished with living and had taken to her bed, where she pretty much spent her whole day. I was even surprised she was at the dinner table that night. Years later I realized she'd only been sixty when she made that decision. These days, sixty's not so old anymore, and you've got plenty of life ahead of you. As I think back, though, she sure seemed older than sixty.

Anyway, she didn't hear a thing, and then they all looked at Poppy.

"Oh, for heavensake," he said, as he often did, "why would they kill a man right in the alley, on the bocce ball court?"

"Arrogance, Mr. Velez," O'Connor said. "We're pretty sure we know who did, and by leavin' the body on the court he's pretty much tellin' us he did it, but we have no proof. So we need a witness in order to arrest him."

We all knew he was talking about Mr. DiCicca and that nobody in that neighborhood was going to snitch on him—although I knew because I'd actually seen him do it.

"Well, I don' see nothin'," Poppy said.

Next they all looked at my sister, Linda. She was four years older than I was, which made her nine.

"Mom?" she said.

"It's okay, dear," my mother said. "Just tell the detective what you saw or didn't see."

"Or heard," O'Connor added.

"I didn't see or hear anything," Linda said. "I was asleep."

And so it became my turn. They all turned and looked at me, and I saw something in my mother's eyes. She had found the dirt and twigs in my bed that morning and asked me about it. I had shrugged, flat-out lied and said I didn't know it had gotten there.

"This isn't the end of this, young man," she'd said. "I'll find out how you got your bed so dirty."

Now she stared at me and I thought she knew. In my mind, if she said anything, we'd all be dead.

"Well, son?" Detective O'Connor asked. "Did you see or hear anything last night?"

I stared at him, then at my father, and then my mother. In that moment I swore she shook her head at me. Don't say anything, she was telling me. Don't.

"Bobby?" my father said. "Answer the man."

I turned and looked at the detective. Twenty four hours ago I probably would have been more afraid of him than of old Mr. DiCicca. On that morning, it was no contest.

"I didn't see anything," I said.

The detective must have seen something in my face, though, because he didn't seem to believe me.

He crouched down in front of me and asked, "You didn't see anything?"

"No, sir."

"Or hear anything?"

"No, sir."

"Now son," he said, "if you did see something you should tell me. It's the right thing to do."

"Yes, sir."

"So … did you see anything?"

I hesitated, swallowed and said, "No, sir, I didn't see anything."

O'Connor stood up, looked at my Dad, and then jerked his head at him. They went to the kitchen with the uniformed cop.

My mother looked at me and smiled, and I knew I had done the right thing for my family.

Later, when I went to bed, I could hear my mother and father talking in their room. I couldn't understand the words, but I could hear the murmur of their voices, and knew she was telling him about the dirt and twigs in my bed. I knew my father would agree with my mother, and when I went to sleep I felt safe,

But it wasn't over yet.

3

The next morning there was a pounding on the door. It woke me up, but I didn't get out of bed. I heard voices, and then my father was at my door.

"Bobby, come with me."

I got out of bed and walked over to him. He put his hand on my shoulder and said, "Don't be afraid, all right?"

"All right."

We walked into the living room, in the front of the house where we lived. My grandmother and grandfather were not there. Neither was my sister. Just me, my mother and my father. Also there were four men. Two I didn't recognize, but the other two I did. One was Vito, and the other was old Mr. DiCicca.

" ... telling you, Mrs. Ravisi, there is a-nothin' to worry about," he was saying. "We just wanna talk to the boy."

"I don't understand, Mr. DiCicca—"

My mother stopped short as my father and I came into the room. Vito turned and glared at me. Although I had never seen the faces of the other two men in the alley, I was sure these were them. They stared at me with cold eyes.

Mr. DiCicca looked down at me and smiled. In the yellow light from the two lamps in the living room his skin still looked like sandpaper to me. He looked like old Mr. DiCicca to me, the Bocce

Ball King of Farragut Road, but I remembered what he had looked like to me that night, from my hiding place in the bushes, and I felt my blood go cold. Even at the tender young age of five I knew that, at that moment, my entire family was in danger.

"Mr. DiCicca," my father said. "This is Bobby."

"Hello, Bobby," DiCicca said. "You know who I am?"

I nodded. "Mr. DiCicca."

He laughed.

"All-a you children, you call me old Mr. DiCicca, or old man DiCicca, don't-a you?" he asked.

"I call you Mr. DiCicca," I said, and then hastily added, "sir."

Suddenly, the old man's face went cold, and I knew I'd blown it. He knew what the kids called him, and claiming that I didn't was the wrong move.

"Joey," he said, to my father, "dress the boy."

"What for?"

"I'm-a gonna take him to the luncheonette for an egg cream."

"This early in the morning?" my mother asked.

He looked at my mother and smiled.

"There are certain advantages to being as old as I am, Mrs. Ravisi," he said. Oddly, that whole sentence came out without an accent. Years later I wondered if the entire accent had been a put on.

He turned and looked at me.

"We are gonna go for a egg cream, and a talk, eh, Bobby? Like two men?"

"Yes, sir."

"Go ahead, Bobby," my father said. "Get dressed."

I pulled on a T-shirt, jeans, and my Keds with shaking fingers and returned to the living room. It never occurred to me to run out the back door.

" … better happen to my son, Mr. DiCicca," my father was saying to the old man when I returned. "Remember that."

"Joey, Joey," DiCicca said, "you gotta nothin' to worry about, eh?" He patted my father's cheek like a kindly old uncle.

"Joe—" my mother started, but my father said, "Hush."

He squatted in front of me and said, "Mr. DiCicca's going to take you for an egg cream, and a talk, Bobby. You tell him what he wants to know, all right?"

"Yes, sir."

He took me by the shoulders. "Everything will be all right."

I nodded.

"Come on, kid," Vito said, and reached for me.

"Vito!" the old man snapped. "You don't-a touch the boy."

Vito stepped back as if scalded.

"You come-a with me, Bobby," DiCicca said. "My friends, they gonna stay with you family until we get back."

"Yes, sir."

The old man and I went out the front door. Right around the corner from us was a luncheonette, where most of us kids went for candy and soda and, when we had enough money, an egg cream or milk shake, maybe a vanilla soda.

"You go to school, Bobby?" he asked, while we walked.

"No, sir."

"How old are you?"

"Five."

"And no school?"

"I'm gonna start kindergarten when the summer is over."

"Ah, kindergarten," he said. "You afraid?"

I might have been, but suddenly kindergarten didn't seem all that scary.

"No, sir."

"Good, good," he said. "You are a brave little boy."

When we got to the luncheonette the busiest part was the window, where people stopped and bought the newspaper. Inside, the metal stools with the red seats were empty. Usually, there were people having breakfast, but not on this morning.

"Good morning, Mr. DiCicca," the man behind the counter said, almost bowing.

"Good morning, Frank," DiCicca said. "Come on, Bobby. Up-a you go."

With surprising strength the old man lifted me onto a stool, and then sat next to me.

"Coffee, Mr. DiCicca?' Frank asked.

"No. My young friend and me, we gonna have egg creams this morning. What flavor you like, Bobby?"

I liked strawberry milk shakes a lot better than egg creams, loved watching the man scoop the milk, ice cream, and syrup into the metal cup and force it onto the pistachio green Hamilton mixer. I even loved the roar it made as it blended the shake. But I didn't want to make Mr. DiCicca mad. I'd already made one misstep.

"Chocolate," I said.

"Two chocolate egg creams, Frank."

I occupied myself watching Frank make the egg creams, studied him rapidly stirring the long silver spoon as he poured the seltzer into the syrup and milk. He slid the two frothy-topped glasses onto the counter in front of us and placed a straw next to each.

"Thank-a you, Frank."

Frank simply nodded and withdrew.

"Go ahead," DiCicca told me, "drink your egg cream."

I took a sip, wishing it was a strawberry shake.

"So, Bobby," the old man said, "did what you saw the other night scare you?"

Briefly, I thought about lying to him, but I must have been one smart five year old because I decided that wouldn't do any good.

"Yes, sir."

"That's good," he said. "It was a terrible thing. You should be scared. Did-a you tell your parents what-a you saw?"

"No."

"And the police? When they came to your house last night? What did you tell them?"

"Nothin'."

"Nothing at all?"

"No, sir."

"Why not?"

I took a sip from my drink before answering him.

"I didn't want to."

He drank from his own glass, just one sip, then pushed it away.

"I'm-a not supposed to have egg creams," he said. "They're a-no good for me."

I didn't say anything.

"If I drink them, they will a-kill me," he said. "You shouldn't drink anything, or do anything, that would-a get you killed. Do you understand?"

"Yes, sir."

He reached out and tousled my hair, which was still a mess from sleeping.

"You a good boy," he said. "Finish-a you drink and I take-a you home."

🌿

When we got home my father and mother were sitting with Vito and the other two men in the living room. They were all quiet, and looked at Mr. DiCicca as we entered.

"Come," he said to his men. "We are finished here."

"But, Don—" Vito started.

The old man cut him off with a wave of his hand.

"We are leaving," he said. "Go!"

The other two men went out the front door without a word. Vito dragged his feet, but finally he left too.

"Joey, Rose," DiCicca said, "you have a good-a boy, here. From now on, for as long as you a-live in this neighborhood, you will never have to lock-a you doors again. *Ciao.*"

After DiCicca and his men left my mother and father looked at me. My father asked, "What did you see, Bobby?"

I hesitated. I realized I knew something that could get my family killed—but only I knew it, and I wasn't going to say a word. If I told my father and mother, then they would know too.

"Nothin'," I said, "I didn't see nothin'."

☆

It only took a month for my father to find us a house in a newly developed section of Canarsie and move us out of that neighborhood. He stopped playing poker with the old Italian men and I never saw a bocce ball match again.

JUST OFF
THE BOAT

SUNSET
SJ ROZAN

THAT NIGHT, LUCAS CHEN WAS LOSING.

Not a new experience; you gamble, sometimes you lose. He wasn't used to losing this big, though, or having his IOU's held by a man who cut off your toes if you stiffed him.

"Hot in here." He ran his finger inside his collar.

Qiu, across the table, squinted against cigarette smoke. "Not for winners." Chips clattered as he raked them in.

Lucas was playing poker in Wong's basement betting parlor, because he'd already lost at fan-tan, and yesterday at dice. "Wong!" He ignored Qiu. "You have air conditioning, or not?"

"How I supposed pay electrical bill, guys like you got so big markers?"

They had to speak English, Wong being an FOB Beijinger and Lucas an ABC from Cantonese stock. But Lucas and Wong understood each other well enough.

"How'm I supposed to see my cards through the sweat dripping in my eyes?"

"Maybe, you don't see cards, you bet smarter. Getting tired carrying you, boy." But Wong went to the wall and turned a dial. Overhead ducts rumbled.

"Doesn't seem to be your night, Lucas." Shoemaker Kee spoke mildly as he thumbed his cards apart. "Maybe you should pack it in."

Lucas had known Shoemaker Kee all his life. Shoemaker Kee and Lucas's Auntie Chen came over from China as six-year-olds, met on Eighth Avenue the day their families moved in. Back then not so many Chinese lived in Sunset Park.

Shoemaker Kee threw a chip in the pot. "You planning on gambling away all Auntie Chen's good luck?"

"What luck's that?" Qiu saw the bet.

"Forget it." Lucas raised. "She's not interested."

"In what?" Qiu kept at it.

"She's had a big offer on her house." Shoemaker Kee watched his new card land. To Lucas: "She's not selling?"

"No chance."

Lucas played a few more hands, winning once, folding early on his own deal, and losing twice. "Damn." He leaned his chair back and called over his shoulder. "Wong, I'm all in."

"You think I care?"

"I'm changing tables. I need a new stake."

"Don't push me, boy."

"Takes money to make money."

Lucas went with Wong into the back, came out with a note, gave it to Alicia—Wong's daughter, the only woman allowed in the basement parlor, and only to pass out chips—and took his new fistful of reds, whites, and blues across the room. Wide pipes and narrow conduit hugged the ceiling. Sometimes they gurgled as something rushed to or from the dumpling house upstairs. Lucas wondered what the racket would be like if you could hear money flowing into and out of gambler's pockets. And always the steady drip, drip as Wong took his cut. Wong never got involved in anything if he didn't get a cut.

He made his way to the corner table. "Room for one more?"

"Especially you, I hear you're losing." Jimmie Louie scraped his chair over to make room. "How much you down over there?" They spoke in Cantonese. No newcomers at this table.

"Ten thousand."

"*Ten?* Wong let you get that deep?"

Lucas laughed. "I'm in way deeper than that. Bad luck for the last two, three weeks. But that streak's about to break."

Linton Pang shuffled the cards. "I heard you're into Wong for close to six figures." Even sitting, Pang towered over everyone. He was another friend of Auntie Chen's. Their families, from the same village near Guangzhou, had come to America together. They'd been expected to marry, but Auntie had been swept off her feet by Xu Chen, dead now six years. Pang had stayed single his whole life.

Lucas stacked chips. "Can't break a streak if you don't play."

Pang shook his head. "Hate to see Auntie Chen lose another one."

"Don't worry about my Auntie."

"No?" Pang passed the deck to fat Tom Long. "How's your cousin Donnie?"

Lucas scowled. "Donnie's in Guangzhou. Needed a change."

"Hope he likes it there."

Lucas didn't answer.

"Donnie Chen's in China?" Tom Long, always cheerful but never the swiftest, dealt cards around the table. "I wondered why I hadn't seen him around."

Pang eyed Lucas."He hasn't been around. He owes First Zhang forty thousand dollars."

Long's smile faded. First Zhang, the moneylender, got his name at birth to mark his parents' hopes for many sons. He used it now to remind clients of the necessary order of settling debts. When Pang spoke his name everyone fell silent. At least Wong only cut off debtors' toes.

"Donnie's over there trying to get rich." Lucas shrugged off Pang's tone. "It's glorious, so they say."

"He can't come back." Pang put it plainly.

Lucas looked at his cards. "Auntie Chen could bring him back if she weren't pig-headed."

"Sure." Jimmie Louie threw in his hand. "She'll just take forty thousand dollars out of the rice bag."

"There's interest on that." Pang scowled. "It'll be up around sixty thousand by now."

Lucas threw in his cards, too. "She could sell that rat-trap house for six times that."

They all looked confused: Pang, and Long, and Jimmie Louie, and the two others, men named Woo and Ko whom Lucas didn't know well. Lucas surveyed them. "She had an offer! Turned it down, the crazy old bird."

"For that house, for that kind of money?" Woo's eyes widened. He lived a street over from Auntie Chen, in a better house.

"Two seventy-five. They would've gone three twenty-five, three fifty, no problem."

"Hey." Ko slapped his cards down. "Are we playing poker or telling real estate jokes?"

They played out the hand and dealt the next one. "That house can't be worth anything near that." Woo, picking up his cards, shook his head. "Ling just sold on my street for one forty."

"And Auntie Chen's can't be worth even that." Jimmie Louie backed Woo up. "It has bad plumbing. The roof sags. Hasn't been painted in years. Anyway, I heard she got a bank loan on it after Donnie got in trouble with First Zhang."

Pang gave Jimmie Louie a patient look. "If she'd done that, why would Donnie still be in China?"

"And who'd want that house anyway?" Woo was dismissive.

Lucas looked up from his shrunken pile of chips. "You don't know?"

"Know what?"

"Who wants it."

"What are you talking about?"

"Trump."

"Trump?" Woo blinked.

"He wants that whole corner. The four houses east of Moon Garden, and the empty lot behind. The other three've already agreed in principle to sell—Lau, and Big Di, in the middle house, and Little Di, his son next door. But if Auntie Chen doesn't sell, the whole plan's screwed. That's why they've gone so high."

"Small lot, even combined." Pang frowned. "What would Trump want it for?"

"A vertical mall." Lucas was enjoying the looks on their faces. "Like Hong Kong. First one in New York."

"That's crazy. In Sunset Park? It'll never work."

"Maybe not. So what? He's Trump. He'll make money, whatever happens."

"Yeah." Ko looked at his own diminished chip pile. "How does he do that?"

"Uses other people's money." Pang rearranged his cards. "If this is true, it must be some Chinese investor. One of those new rich. Who else would buy such a dumb idea?"

"Like I say, it's glorious." Lucas leaned back. "The new rich in China have money to burn."

"How do you know this?" Woo was unconvinced. "About Trump."

Lucas allowed himself a small smile. "Janey See. From Forty-sixth Street? She works at City Planning. Paperwork came across her desk. She shouldn't have told me, but … "

"Yeah, you're irresistible." Ko, who rented, was clearly bored. "You in or out?"

Lucas played the hand and lost. Woo handed him the cards for the next deal. "But Auntie Chen won't sell?"

"You can't get over this, can you?" Lucas grinned. "No, Auntie says she grew up there. Says it's home."

"She's always talking about going back to China." Jimmie Louie shuffled the second deck. "Doesn't she still own a house there?"

"In her home village." Lucas dealt the cards. "Which is mine, too, by the way."

"The house?"

"No, idiot. The village." Lucas wouldn't have called any other man at the table 'idiot.' Pang, he knew for certain, wasn't one, and Woo and Ko and fat Tom Long were from Pang and Auntie's generation. But he was older than Jimmie Louie. "The house is Auntie's. Where she was born."

"And she's always talking about going back there." Jimmie Louie collected his cards.

"Yeah, well, I guess talk is cheap. She's been here since she was six. Which is about a hundred years now, right, Pang?"

Pang gave a philosophical grunt.

"Don't you own a house in that village, too?" Woo turned to Pang.

"Mud walls and broken tiles." Pang didn't look up from his cards. "Maybe Trump wants that, too. I'll call him in the morning."

Woo laughed.

"Can we play?" Ko gave an exasperated sigh.

Lucas scowled. "Only if I dealt myself a hand worth playing."

But he hadn't, and neither, it seemed, did anyone else. Lucas, tapped out, left soon after.

Auntie Chen's plump form was curled in front of the TV when he came in. She stirred and sat up.

"Have you eaten?"

"Yes, Auntie. Go back to sleep."

"How did your evening go?"

"Very well." Lucas started up the rickety stairs. "Very well."

🌿

The next night Lucas took Janey See to dinner at Moon Garden.

"I got a strange call at work." Janey bit a tiny hole in a soup dumpling and drew out the broth. "A reporter from the *Sunset News*. Fred Cho. Said he was following a story about Trump buying up property in Sunset Park."

"Really? What'd you say?"

"That it was against policy to discuss pending matters."

Lucas nodded.

"But here's the strange part. There's no Fred Cho at the *Sunset News*."

"Is that a fact?" Lucas ran an eye over the menu. "Let's have pea shoots, what do you say?"

✼

The following morning Big Di, cutting his roses, called to Lucas. "I saw Alicia Wong yesterday."

"Really?"

"Yes. She complimented my roses and asked if it was true I was selling the house. What a shame, she said, to leave such a garden."

"What did you tell her?"

"I said I'd had an inquiry, but one always has inquiries. But if the price were good enough, I said, I'd be interested. A man of my age has to look ahead."

"What did she say?"

"She asked about my son. She said she'd heard he was selling, too. I said, if my son and his family were to move, what would keep me here?"

"Interesting." Lucas sniffed a rose. "The yellow ones are spectacular, Mr. Di."

✼

Late that afternoon Lucas ran into Shoemaker Kee outside the fishmonger's. "Lucas! Guess who's having tea at the Cloud Pavilion."

"Mao's ghost?"

"First Zhang. And Wong."

"Together?"

Shoemaker Kee nodded vigorously.

"Hmm." Lucas inspected the bins of fish. "What looks good to you? Auntie wanted perch, but they're out."

✼

Over the next two days rumors flew in Sunset Park: that Auntie Chen had turned down a big offer on her house. And that Lucas Chen was into Wong for a hundred thousand dollars. People asked

Auntie Chen about the offer and got a shrug. No one asked Lucas about the debt because some things are bad luck even to know. Some people eyed him strangely—in Sunset Park luck was considered contagious, like disease or a laughing fit—but as long as he paid cash no one turned him away.

⚜

Until the second night, when he knocked on the door of Wong's gambling parlor. Alicia opened the peephole and spoke through the rusted grate. "Papa says no."

"What do you mean, no?"

"Papa says he's calling in his marker."

Lucas stood open-mouthed. "He can't."

"Yes, he can. You owe him too much money. I'm sorry, Lucas." She closed the grate.

Lucas turned and walked slowly up the stairs, wondering if Alicia apologized to everyone whose toes Wong was about to chop off.

⚜

The next morning Sunset Park buzzed with the news of the pair of toeless Nikes found on Auntie Chen's doorstep.

⚜

That afternoon Lucas found himself beside stone-faced Auntie Chen in the teashop back room First Zhang used as an office.

"Your son already took off with forty thousand dollars of mine." First Zhang sipped tea. Auntie Chen slurped hers. Lucas left his on the desk. "Why should I lend more to your deadbeat nephew?"

"Not to him." Auntie Chen threw Lucas a scowl. "To me."

"It's only out of respect, Auntie Chen, that I haven't demanded you pay your son's debt." First Zhang turned his soft look on Lucas. "Or that you pay it."

"With what?"

"With whatever you were using to stake yourself at Wong's."

"Wong staked me."

"So much money. It's unlike Wong. He's slipping. Did you think of finding a job?"

"When my company's manufacturing moved to China the accounting jobs moved, too." Lucas was aware of sounding defensive. "No one seems to need accountants right now."

"Lazy boy." Auntie Chen muttered.

First Zhang held up his hand for quiet. He sipped tea again, closing his eyes. When he was done he put the cup gently down. "I won't lend you money, Auntie Chen. You couldn't possibly meet my terms."

"You didn't have the same worry about my son."

"Your son had a job. A car. Prospects. He seemed like a reasonable risk."

"A job? He's a carpenter! And he's too young. You should have turned him away."

"How was I to know he'd run? Anyway, I hope he's getting rich over there, because I expect to be paid, with interest, when he comes back."

"He's not coming back."

"Oh, Auntie Chen, of course he is. This is his home. Everyone wants to go home. But let's not discuss Donnie. As to your request: All respect, Auntie Chen, but you are not a good risk."

"I—"

"No, no. No argument. No loan. But I'll buy your house."

Auntie Chen stared. "My house? It's not for sale."

"It's your only asset. How would you have guaranteed my loan, except with your house?"

"I hadn't—"

"Thought about that? No, I know you hadn't. Come, Auntie Chen. I won't insult you with a low offer. I know what's going on. I'll give you a hundred and twenty-five thousand dollars."

"But my house ... "

Lucas spoke up loudly. "If you know what's going on, you know that Auntie's been offered twice that already. And that the … other bidder … will go much higher."

Auntie Chen glared. First Zhang smiled. "Yes, but transactions like that take time. If Wong is calling in his marker on you, Lucas, you might want this completed sooner rather than later." He dropped his gaze to Lucas's polished wing-tips.

Lucas clamped his jaw shut and didn't answer.

"Two hundred fifty." Auntie Chen spoke suddenly.

Both men turned to her.

"You're so smart." She glowered at First Zhang. "You drove my son away. All I have left is this fool nephew." She drilled a look into Lucas, then went on. "You can have the house. But you can't steal it. Two hundred and fifty thousand."

Lucas watched the abacus spinning behind First Zhang's eyes. "Donnie's debt comes out of that. You'll get one hundred and fifty."

"Donnie only borrowed forty!"

"There's interest."

"Not that much!" Auntie Chen's hard stare did battle with First Zhang's soft eyes. "I get two hundred twenty."

"One seventy."

"Two ten."

"One eighty."

"Two hundred!"

First Zhang smiled indulgently. "All right, Auntie Chen. Out of respect."

"Cash." Auntie Chen sat back. "Wong's impatient."

⚕

The next morning Lucas accompanied Auntie Chen to bring a deed and bill of sale to First Zhang.

"My lawyer will take care of the rest of the paperwork and be in touch, Auntie Chen." First Zhang smiled magnanimously and handed Lucas a nylon bag. Lucas unzipped it, saw it was full of cash, and zipped it again.

"You're not going to count it?" First Zhang looked surprised.

"Did you expect me to?"

"Of course."

"Then I'm sure it's all here."

Auntie Chen turned to leave.

Lucas lingered. "Satisfy my curiosity, Zhang. It was your idea for Wong to call in my marker, right? You'd heard the rumors about Auntie's house?"

Zhang gave Lucas his gentle smile. "Try not to gamble anymore, Lucas. You're not very good. It was Wong's idea. He suggested that, for a consideration, he might do me that service."

Lucas nodded and left.

⚘

That evening, Lucas helped Auntie Chen get comfortable.

"Stop laughing at me, you useless boy."

"I can't help it." He tried to supress a smile. "Your feet don't reach the floor."

"We should have flown coach. The seats are smaller."

"All the way to Guangzhuo? What kind of a celebration would that be?" He handed her a champagne glass from the flight attendant's tray. "Auntie, you were great."

Auntie Chen reclined her seat. "Don't you think we should have given Pang more?"

"He got the same as everyone else." Lucas spoke patiently; they'd had this discussion before."Five thousand is more than enough."

"For Janey, and Shoemaker Kee, and Big Di, yes." She sipped champagne. "And Lau, and Little Di. They didn't even do anything."

"But they had to be ready, in case."

"Yes, I know. But Wong got twice as much!"

"*Plus* his cut from the four thousand I lost in his basement." Lucas sighed. "*Plus* his 'consideration' from First Zhang. But there was no way he'd have spread the fake story of how much I owed him, or gone to First Zhang to suggest calling in my marker, for less."

"I know. But Pang … "

"Auntie, you're being sentimental. Also silly. He'll be over in the spring, once Donnie gets his house fixed up. If you still want to, you can give him more then. Would you like a pillow?" He plumped one for her. "I'm just sorry we won't see First Zhang's face when his lawyer tells him about the bank loan. And when Trump tells him he never heard of Sunset Park."

"Pah." Auntie Chen snorted. "Why do you need to see his face? You've already seen his money."

"Auntie, you're very wise. As always."

Auntie Chen tucked her legs under her. "Are you sure you have time to come to the village before your job begins?"

"You always have to worry about something, don't you?" Lucas smiled fondly. "I told the firm I could only relocate to China if I could take a few weeks to get settled. They're fine with that."

Auntie Chen also smiled. "I can't wait to see Donnie again."

"He sure sounds happy there." Lucas slid the blind down; they were flying into the sunset.

"I knew he'd like it." Auntie Chen finished her champagne. "You'll like it to. After all, it's your home village. Everyone wants to go home."

HIT AND RUN
GLENVILLE LOVELL

SHE COULD TASTE THE SOURNESS OF HIS kiss long after they made love. If you could call it making love. Thank goodness it lasted no longer than the time it took Carl Lewis to run the hundred meters in the Olympics. As it was, this … lovemaking happened only once; still for weeks she shuddered whenever the thought crossed her mind. It wasn't just the tartness of his breath that repulsed her; his whole body had the sweaty taint of the islands.

The marriage had been arranged by her cousin, Martha, who'd met him in Sin City on Rutland Road where Martha danced three nights a week.

Carla wasn't at all interested when her cousin first broached the subject. This island-man (Martha's term), named Joshua, was offering fifteen thousand dollars to any woman who'd marry him so he could get his green card. With a mouth faster than an Indy race car, Martha had given the man her telephone number, telling him she'd be perfect.

"Girl, you must be crazy, turning down that kinda money," Martha fumed, when Carla explained that she'd refused Joshua's offer. "It ain't like you be rolling in cheddar, sister-girl. Think of all that money you be spending to keep your granny in the nursing home. And it don't look like she gonna be checking out anytime soon. If I wasn't already married I'd grab it and run like a thief. Now that there is the definition of free money."

Joshua called back the next day. Her voice fascinated him, he said. The offer ballooned to thirty thousand dollars. This made her laugh. Was this man for real? And she was suddenly intrigued. As much by the money as by the thought of doing something completely outside her nature. Perhaps Martha wasn't the only one in the family with a wild side.

Would he really pay that kind of money to marry her? Dollar signs began floating in her head. She decided to roll the dice.

"Fifty thousand," she countered.

"Fifty? That's no problem."

"How about seventy-five, then?"

His voice had an exotic polish. "You already said fifty."

"I changed my mind."

"You can't do that."

"Seventy-five. Take it or leave it."

"Seventy-five. But that's final."

"What do you do for a living?" she asked.

"I'm a designer."

"Like in clothes?"

"Furniture."

"Where do you work?"

"I'm self-employed. My designs are one of a kind."

"Have you designed for anybody famous?"

"For the right price, I'll design for anyone."

"Would you design a bed for me?"

"I'm sure you're as lovely as your voice. And I'm not one to turn down a beautiful woman. It'd be a pleasure to make a bed for you."

The deal was consummated the next week at a Caribbean restaurant on Church Avenue, an hour-long meeting over fried chicken and callaloo.

He was very short, much shorter than any man she'd ever gone out with and way shorter than any man she would've thought of giving a second look, but he dressed well. Anyway, this was strictly business. Other than that there was nothing extraordinary about him. Then he took off his gloves and pulled up the sleeves of his bright red sweater and she saw the jewelry.

"Is that a real diamond ring?" she asked.

"Yes."

"And that watch … Is that a Rolex?"

"I believe it is."

"How much? … The two?"

"I don't know. Both gifts … From clients."

The chicken and callaloo were too spicy for her. She'd never had callaloo before, but he told her it tasted like spinach. It didn't. It was slimy and disgusting. As she picked at the chicken for half an hour, he prattled on about all the places he'd visited. Ask her to repeat anything he said and she wouldn't have been able to. She wasn't really listening. Her mind was focused on what she would do with her seventy-five thousand dollars. And after seeing the bank on his arm she was even contemplating asking for another twenty-five thousand.

She sipped her ginger beer and studied his soft, almost soggy eyes. He had long spike-like eyelashes, the kind many women would kill for. And for some reason she found herself smiling at the dark irony of that thought. How shallow to think that a woman would kill to get long eyelashes.

After the waiter had cleared the table Joshua reached into his jacket hanging on the back of the chair and pulled out a large brown envelope which he pushed across the table.

"Forty thousand," he said with a soft smile.

"That wasn't the deal."

"Down payment. The rest you will get when we pick up the marriage license."

She squeezed the envelope and exalted at the firmness of the compacted bills. "In that case you'd better add an extra twenty-five."

He leaned close to her, letting his callaloo breath smack her face. "Greed is not a good thing, you know."

"Neither is lying. You said I'd get all the money today."

He fell back at her reproach. "You've got a beautiful nose."

"Don't try to sweet talk me. Twenty-five more or the deal is off."

His expression turned ugly. "You can't do that."

She thrust the envelope back at him and stood up.

"Okay," he said.

She sat down. "Okay? What does that mean?"

"Twenty-five thousand more. How do I know you're not going to change your mind again?"

"You don't."

Before they left the restaurant he went over the list of things they needed to do for their marriage to appear legitimate for the immigration exam.

Open a joint bank account.

Give each other presents.

Study each other's habits.

Life insurance policies.

"Life insurance?" she asked.

"Yes. I've been told that goes over very well. The bigger the better."

"How much?"

"One million … Each."

"Each?"

"A million on you … A million on me."

"Are you serious?"

"Never more."

The day after they got hitched at City Hall he opened a joint bank account and took out two one-million dollar life insurance policies; one for her and one for him, with the other named as beneficiary.

The thought that she could become a millionaire if her 'husband' died made her giddy. What would it be like to be a millionaire? Freed from the slog of commuting to New Jersey from Brooklyn to that shitty job at Discount Phone Card's customer service desk. Freed from staring at those stale gray walls which she knew was shortening her life. At the very least it was dulling her self esteem.

Freed from obnoxious, pre-Alzheimer fuckers who bombarded her with calls every day simply because they couldn't figure out how to scratch a phone card to find their pin numbers.

One million dollars. She'd be rich. She could bring her granny home from the home and hire a nurse to take care of her. If only this man would pass away before they divorced. It wouldn't bother her none if he simply dropped dead. Free money. Isn't that what Martha called it?

But that was wishful thinking. He was a relatively young man, in his thirties. Chances were he wouldn't die from natural causes any time soon. An accident, perhaps? She read the policy over and over, every fine-printed word. Yes, she'd receive full benefits in case of accidental death.

At first, she felt guilty that she wished for his death. But death was inevitable, she assuaged herself. We all have to die some day. She did not wish for her mother do die, but she did anyway, leaving her with a grandmother to care for and little money. Sometimes she wished that her grandmother would die. There was something liberating about admitting that to herself. Yes, her death and her husband's too, would solve a lot of her problems. Did that make her a bad person?

It was the sex that made up her mind. A man who made love like that didn't deserve to live. You'd think that being short and ugly would force a man to become more skilled in pleasing a woman. Not this muthafucker. He had no clue about the female body.

She hadn't intended to sleep with him and had made up her mind not to encourage him, though he was always complimenting her looks. Business and pleasure didn't mix, her Barbadian grandmother always used to say.

After the marriage he kept asking about moving in together. She was skeptical about this, especially since he would never take her to his apartment.

One night he took her to an African dance concert at Brooklyn College. By the time the fifteen half-naked dancers had wriggled and pranced their way though the two-hour concert, she was so mesmerized that she might've let King Kong ride her booty.

It was probably the worst decision she'd ever made. The first kiss made her skin walk. And it didn't get any better. He nutted in ten seconds flat. She might've forgiven him if he'd been willing to go down on her afterwards. He declared that was something he never did. Men in his culture didn't do that.

The mechanic who fixed her car was an ex-con whom she'd allowed to beat the cakes a while back. He'd pulled some big numbers upstate for armed robbery and her pussy was the first he'd tasted when he got out. To this day he was still grateful and would do anything for her.

He agreed to do the job for five thousand dollars. One Friday night, they got together around midnight in the back of his jeep parked on Rockaway Boulevard to work out the details.

"I think a hit and run accident would be best," she said.

"Yeah. But I gotta get him clean," Kenjo said.

"He goes to Sin City every Saturday night. Around twelve or so. He parks his Beemer in a lot a block away and has to walk back. It's a deserted street. You could wait for him."

""You said his name was Joshua?"

"Yes."

"And he's short? Very short? With eyelashes like a woman's?"

"Yes."

"You sure he's a furniture designer?" the mechanic asked.

"That's what he said."

"I think I know this dude."

"From where?"

"He might be a designer, but not furniture."

"What do you mean?"

"He designs death."

"He designs death? What're you talking about?"

"He does body work for a drug outfit in Brownsville."

"He's a paid killer? … You're kidding, right?"

"Dead … Sorry … No. And I don't think he needs a green card either."

"He's from the islands. He's got an accent."

"True that. But from what I know he was born here. His parents are from the islands. They sent him back when he was a baby to be raised by his grandmother. He's a citizen. Just like you and me."

"Then why did he pay to marry me?"

"You're a pretty woman. He's a frog. Maybe he thinks you'll turn him into a prince."

She tried to laugh, but all she managed was a stilted cough. "You think … " The words stuck in her craw.

Kenjo lit up a big fatty, then finished the thought for her. "A million dollars. I guess he's thinking the same thing you are."

She coughed again and turned her face away from the smoke, resting her head on the dash and closing her eyes. Kenjo massaged her neck. His hands felt like sandpaper. A deep and utter dread sank into her. She removed his hand and lifted up, staring into the darkness ahead.

The street was deserted. Soon time for her to go back into the bar across the street where she served drinks to make extra money. She pondered her fucked-up situation. Married to a killer who was probably at that moment thinking of a way to get rid of her. How would he do it? Hire one of his business colleagues to fit her toe-tag? From here on, she figured, it'd be a game of cat and mouse. She thought of not going back to the apartment. But where would she go? She couldn't go to Immigration because he was a citizen. And she had no proof to take to the police.

She took Kenjo's hand and held it tight. "You think you could still do the job knowing who he is?"

"He ain't no blood of mine," her mechanic said. "Just tell me when."

"Tomorrow night."

She got out of the truck and watched it drive away. She stood on the curb, fighting an urge to sit and cry. She bit her lips hard, but her nerves seemed to have shriveled because she felt no pain.

Standing fifteen yards away from the intersection she decided to cross the wide boulevard at that point instead of walking back to the light. When the light turned in her favor she sniffed the cold air and jerked herself into the street.

Halfway across, the bright lights of a car swerving wildly from Clarkson onto Rockaway trapped her in a high-beam glare. It came bounding towards her increasing speed rapidly, its bright lights dazzlingly beautiful. She stopped dead, realizing the car would blow the red light at Winthrop and there was no way she would get across before it reached her.

As the car entered the intersection a truck traveling west on Winthrop flashed into the picture. The two vehicles met in a fury of sound. Her heart was shocked back into motion. She dashed to the other side as the car tumbled to a stop almost twenty yards away. The truck had not stopped. The driver from the car had been thrown from the crumpled heap and lay in the middle of the street.

She pulled out her phone and dialed 911 as she ran to see if the man was still alive.

"What's your emergency?"

"She didn't hear the woman's voice on the other end. Her eyes and mind were fixed on the grotesque figure in the street. Light fell from the streetlamp, splashing his face in luminous purple. Blood rushed from a gaping hole in his skull. His face seemed frozen in a strange smirk.

"What's your emergency?" the emergency dispatcher said again.

She flip-closed the phone.

The man wasn't breathing. Her husband was dead.

Killing
O'MALLEY
BY
TONY SPINOSA

KILLING O'MALLEY
Tony Spinosa

THOUGH ONLY PUSHING FORTY, PETE CONNELL WAS a bitter old fuck. The kind of man to turn the Host into ashes at the touch of his tongue. *Body of Christ, my ass!* He was the worst kind of bitter old fuck, an impotent drunken one, and a liar to boot. His shamed relations claimed a thousand reasons for Pete's sour spirit. Their favorite centering on the horrors of D-Day.

"Oh, poor Peter," they would say. "The war's what done him in. His couldn't take the carnage on the Normandy beaches. His soul simply broke in the face of so much death. And the bottle … It's ruined better men than himself."

An eloquent defense for sure, but utter bullshit. The only sand to have touched Pete's boney white feet had come from Brighton Beach. As for the war, the closest he'd come to D-Day combat was slapping around a two-buck whore in Omaha, Nebraska for laughing at his limp dick. She'd returned the favor by slashing his face with a straight razor.

"Kraut shrapnel!" he'd bark whenever anyone asked about the scar.

Perhaps the weakest excuse of all was the drink. In the overall scheme of things, Pete Connell had brought more troubles to the bottle than the bottle to him. No, some men are just bitter born. He was one. There was but one pleasure, one pure joy in his miserable existence; his beloved Dodgers. Them Bums were it for him. Forget Kelly green Irish blood. Connell bled Brooklyn Dodger blue.

That night at Muldoon's when the news fell on the patrons like a British Comet plummeting out of the sky, Pete was already feeling it. He was several sheets to the wind, beer and bile indistinguishable to his palate. And what made the news unbearable was the messenger who delivered it. Pete Connell despised Michael Duke for everything Duke was and *he* was not.

Whereas Connell had pissed away his police career—taking a five buck bribe and a blow job from a colored whore and getting caught in the act—Duke had built his American dream out of death and dust. Then again, Connell always sold himself cheap. Even now, as the produce manager at the Packers Supermarket on Kings Highway, Pete had sewn the seeds of his own demise. For months he'd been selling a quarter of his daily order to a local green grocer on Avenue P for ten cents on the dollar and putting the shortages down as spoils. Ten cents on the dollar, that said it all about Peter Connell.

Michael Duke had come to the States after the war with the first wave of refugees and camp survivors. When he arrived in Brooklyn in '46, he was Mikhail Dukelsky, a twenty-one-year-old from the outskirts of Kiev who had exploited his wits and math skills to impress his *Einsatz Groupen* masters enough to last three years under their blood red thumbs. He had used his ten years in New York to change more than his name. Now a citizen and a CPA employed by the city, he lived a quiet, comfortable life with his wife and newborn son in a nicely appointed two-bedroom flat on Avenue H. He'd even purchased a plot of land in the Catskills on which he someday hoped to build a summer bungalow.

His one selfish pleasure was his after-dinner stroll to Muldoon's Tavern at the junction of Flatbush and Nostrand Avenues. Mike enjoyed the serenity of the Brooklyn College campus as he made his way to the bar for his nightly stein of Rheingold. It relaxed him, strolling across the peaceful green quadrangle, stopping to gaze up at the clock mounted atop the white steeple. He loved the chiming of the bells. In the Ukraine, there were clock and bell towers too, thousands of them. Not even the Nazis and accursed Soviets could have destroyed them all. But Duke thought the Brooklyn College tower most beautiful of all. It was so un-European, so devoid of religious connotation. That night, however, he did not linger by the clock tower.

"If it ain't Mike the kike," Pete whispered just loud enough for Duke to hear.

Usually, Michael ignored the man's asinine barbs. Compared to the inhumanity he had suffered at the hands of the *SS*, Connell's bigotry was no more than the buzzing of a fly. But just lately, it had begun to eat at him. Maybe it was the birth of his son Alan that had changed his attitude. That he had been forced to endure the hatred of others in the old country was one thing, but this was America, *he* was an American, and Michael would be damned if he would let small-minded cowards like Pete Connell poison his son's life. Tonight, he would see to that.

The bar was empty save for Connell, Muldoon himself, Hattie the Hooker, and the Professor—a bum who had Einstein hair and scribbled nonsense on Bazooka Bubble Gum wrappers.

"Hey, Mikey!" Muldoon brightened, putting up a tall glass of beer. "How goes it?"

"Thank you, Patrick," Duke said, placing two quarters on the bar. "As to your question … I fear it goes not so very well."

"How's that?" the barman asked.

"I bring bad news, terrible news."

"What, someone blow up the Hebrew National hot dog factory?" Connell blurted out, laughing at his own joke.

"Very funny, Pete. Why not cut the man some slack?" Muldoon snapped.

"No, Patrick, that's all right. After I divulge my news, we will all need to find a way to laugh." Duke sipped his beer.

"Now you got me curious, Mikey."

"Yeah, Heeb, you even got my attention."

"Well, you know I work for the City Budget Office, right? And if you recall, a few months back I mentioned I was working on a very serious project that could effect all of Brooklyn."

Muldoon clapped his hands together. "Sure! Sure! But you said it was very hush hush and you couldn't say much about it 'cause it could land you in hot water."

"Yes, Patrick, you remember."

"Enough with the suspense, Heeb," Connell snarled.

"Okay, I guess I should just say it then. The Dodgers are leaving Brooklyn for good."

Connell spit out his drink. Hattie lifted her head off the bar. The Professor stopped scribbling. He never stopped scribbling.

"I like you a lot, Mikey, but you shouldn't oughta joke like that, not if you wanna live to see the sunrise."

"I wish only that it was a joke, Patrick." Duke held his hands prayerfully. "But I swear on the souls of my murdered parents that I speak the truth."

Grief grew heavy in the air as Michael Duke explained how Mayor Wagner tried calling Walter O'Malley's bluff and how O'Malley had, in no uncertain terms, told Wagner to go fuck himself.

"He did a little Irish jig," Mike said, lifting his trouser legs and hopping from foot to foot. "He invited Wagner to come visit him in L.A. and that he would find the mayor some nice seats in the Coliseum with the wetbacks, Chinks and, Japs."

Of course, this last part of Duke's story was a complete fabrication meant specifically for Pete's ears. Mike went on for ten minutes describing in excruciating detail how Mr. O'Malley had taken great pleasure in his own greed and the thought of spitting on all of Brooklyn.

"The things he said … I am embarrassed to even repeat them. I was sick to hear such things."

"Go on," Connell demanded, "tell me what he said."

"First," Mike said, placing a ten spot on the bar, "a round for all of us. You too, Patrick."

"Okay, kike," Pete said after downing a shot of Irish, "let's have it. Every last word."

Mike suggested that he and Pete retire to a corner table to discuss it between themselves. No need to upset anyone else more than they already were. When they got to the table, Mike said he knew that Pete hated him, but that on this issue they were brothers, that tonight all Brooklynites were brothers in grief. Connell grudgingly agreed. Mike waved at Muldoon to keep the drinks coming.

Duke laid it on thick, pulling Pete's strings with every word, whispering so that only the man across the table from him could hear. First he told how O'Malley admitted to always hating guineas, Polacks, Krauts, and spics.

"O'Malley says the only reason he ever let niggers on the team was because the fucking Jew bankers demanded it. But I'm sorry to say, Pete—May I call you Pete?"

Connell nodded.

"I'm sorry to say that O'Malley hates his own people worst of all. He called you all a bunch of stupid micks, donkeys that couldn't think their way out of a potato patch.

Said the Irish who came over after the famine were the dregs of the race, the very worst kind of shanty scum imaginable."

Pete seemed almost in shock. He laid his head down across his folded arms.

"It's okay, Pete," Mike comforted, placing a hand on his shoulder. "Let's get you a double. You need it." He waved at Muldoon.

The barman brought over the drinks. Waiting for Muldoon to retreat to the bar, Duke suggested to his new found friend that they compose a letter to the Dodgers' owner.

"You'll speak for all of Brooklyn, Pete, and on my honor, I will hand deliver the letter to Mr. O'Malley tomorrow."

"Hey, nut job!" Connell barked at the Professor. "Gimme your fucking pen or I'll snap your neck like a toothpick!"

The nervous little man ran out the door, dropping his pen at Connell's feet as he passed. Mike leaned down to retrieve the pen and then unfurled a bar napkin. He wrote as Pete Connell spewed out a stream of curses that would make a tombstone blush. Muldoon tried to listen, but couldn't make out a word. Ten minutes and another round later, Mike Duke stood up and placed the napkin in his back pocket.

"Goodnight, Pete. Again, I'm sorry for this terrible news."

"Yeah, sure. You jus' remember t'do wha' you promised with tha' note," Connell slurred.

Mike hesitated. "I'm sorry, Pete. I can't do that. You couldn't have meant what you had me write down. In a day or two, you might feel differently and—"

"Gimme tha' fuckin' letta, ya kike, or I'll finish wha' the Nazis couldn't!"

Mike shrugged his shoulders. Dutifully, he handed the folded napkin to Pete who made a show of balling it up and shoving it into his jacket pocket.

"Now *gedthafugouttahere!*"

On his way out, Mike slipped Muldoon another five bucks and told him to keep Pete's drinks coming.

"You're a better man than me, Mikey," Muldoon said.

"I feel sad for him, Patrick. And tonight, we're all in mourning, no? I too am a little *schickered* or I would stay and keep an eye on Pete. He's in such a bad way. Well, goodnight, my friend." He shook the barman's hand and left.

Two hours later, Pete Connell stumbled out of Muldoon's into the moonless night. Using walls, fences, parked cars to keep him upright, he made his way home. He was way too drunk to notice either the cold rain or the man across the street who shadowed his every step and turn. When Connell slipped into a narrow alley between his building and the subway trestle, his shadow closed ground.

"Who'zzz there?"

"It's just me, Pete, your new friend."

"Wha'?"

That word formed Pete Connell's mouth into the perfect shape to receive the barrel of Michael Duke's Luger. Connell froze. That pleased Mike very much, but not quite as much as his timing.

"Do you recognize this pistol?" Mike taunted. "It's the one you took off the dead *Wermacht* captain at Omaha Beach. You tell that story to everyone who comes into Muldoon's. I've heard you tell the story five times in one night. Surely the police will not question its origin when they find it next to your body. The note in your pocket will make mention of it, just in case."

Connell's eyes got wide with fear and sudden comprehension.

"That's right, buddy, not your drunken ravings about killing O'Malley. A suicide note."

As the subway rumbled by, Mike Duke blew Connell's brain out the back of his skull with the Luger *he* had taken off an *SS* captain as the Russians approached his labor camp in the woods outside Kiev. Michael had slit the Nazi's throat and urinated on him as he bled to death. What was that old saying about dancing with the devil? You don't change the devil. The devil changes you.

He did not urinate on Connell's body. Instead he placed the dead man's right hand around the grip of the Luger and let gravity take its course. Then he replaced the note in Pete's pocket with one he had composed as he waited for Connell to emerge from Muldoon's. After calmly checking that things looked just right, Michael Duke walked home to his nicely appointed two bedroom apartment.

There he peeled off his gloves and clothing, patiently throwing them down the incinerator chute one item at a time. He couldn't risk anything getting jammed in the chute. After his shower, Mike stood silent vigil in his son's room, watching the little boy toss and turn in his crib until the sun came up.

At about the same time, the cops were rolling over pete Connell's stiff body and reading the suicide note taken from his pocket. The poor man couldn't bear the thought of the Dodgers moving out of Brooklyn. He didn't want to spend his days pining for his beloved Bums, obsessed with thoughts of killing O'Malley. It was just easier, the note said, to end his *own* life. When news of the Dodgers' pending move broke later that morning, the detectives understood completely. They felt much the same way. All Brooklyn did. That day, Mike Duke was the only happy man in all the borough.

GOOD COPS, BAD COP

BRENDA, MY STAR
Jim Fusilli

WARNEKE WHISTLED, AND THEN HE DROPPED THE newspaper sheet, covering the good-looking colored boy's face. He knew him–Jerome Maddux Jr.: sixteen, long-limbed, coffee-light skin. Heading into senior year at Erasmus High; his father a dentist, which explained the kid's faultless teeth. Junior Maddux, a singer with a honey-smooth voice. Which, Warneke figured, explained the windpipe, crushed now like an old Lilly cup, ragged slits in the flesh on the throat, fresh blood from his mouth on the cracked sidewalk.

Six dollars in his pocket, a learner's permit to drive and Ben Zengelman's business card, fourth letter of the talent agent's last name a G clef.

"Stomped him, Detective," the uniform said, hovering as Warneke lifted off a knee, clapping concrete dust from his hands. "Fuckin' shame, no?"

Warneke left on the Plymouth's high beams, and stark light illuminated the body and half the side street: molting trees behind ankle-high iron work, parked cars, rubbish tossed to the curb; up at the window sills, women in curlers and ratty floral nightgowns resting on elbows and forearms. Gathered outside the four-story brick buildings, portly husbands, gangly husbands; undershirts, slacks retrieved from the backs of chairs, shoes untied; the orange tips of their Luckys, Camels and Viceroys aglow.

His back to Flatbush Avenue, Warneke said, "Who seen nothing?"

"Everybody," the uniform replied, looking at the detective, at the tent-shaped newspaper over Junior Maddux's bloody face. "Everybody seen nothing.

"Warneke absently thumbed the red feather on his straw fedora. Almost midnight on a sticky Friday, and behind him, traffic like it was noon, cars crawling. A horn honked, and a tire squealed as it caught on an old trolley track.

"Nobody heard nothing neither," the uniform added.

Maybe so, Warneke thought, maybe. Maddux walking north along Flatbush, going downtown. Psst, a guy says and the kid turns right. Dull, quivering lamp light obscured by plump leaves. Bang, and down he goes. Stomp. A sickly gurgle as he struggles to breathe, his face turning blue, gasping, thin fingers clawing the air.

"Yeah. A real shame," the uniform mused, pushing back his hat, scratching his flattop. His name was Fitzsimmons, and he had sweat beads on his cheeks. "I mean, the throat, and the new suit and all. Sharkskin, ain't it?"

Yeah, and new: the Robert Hall label below the belt, razor creases on the slacks, length tucked under, safety pins, the vents still sewn with factory thread. The kid bought it today, maybe even earlier tonight. Eight-to-five says his mother told him she'd tailor it tomorrow, but he couldn't wait to show it off.

Warneke had it figured good: Maddux was on his way to the Fox, catching up with friends who knew silver sharkskin meant he was headed right. A year or two, and Zengelman's got him up on the stage, Murray the K calling his name, the orchestra kicking off his hit tune.

"Go to the BMT at Atlantic and walk yourself back here. See who seen him."

Fitzsimmons frowned. "BMT?"

"Kid lived on Cortelyou."

During the war, Junior Maddux's father was a division dental surgeon, and he treated colored soldiers in Saipan, repairing shrapnel-shattered jaws. Walking a beat in Ditmas Park, Warneke knew him enough to nod hello; Warneke, who broke his femur near Barrigada, accounting for the slight limp, the cookie in his shoe. He went to the funeral at the Grand Army Plaza after Maddux got run over by a Buick. His young wife in black, dabbing her eyes with a lace handkerchief and there was Junior holding her hand, chin high, already tall. Singing along with the choir.

Warneke saw in his mind what's next: Althea Maddux arriving, jumping the squad car before it stopped, screaming her boy's name. Cold eyes on her: Them over there, drooped on the window sills, perched on painted steps, each of them thinking the kid had no business here in the first place, no matter what CORE and Kennedy say.

Ready to leave, Warneke threw his thumb over his shoulder.

"Sure. OK," Fitzsimmons replied quick, blinking as he worked through his futile task. Maybe five hundred people on Flatbush Avenue on a Friday near midnight, wishing for a breeze in the August heat. Plus buses stopping every other block, and the news-stands. "Colored boy in a suit, tall, teeth?" Shrugs all around until some penny-ante wise-ass says, "What's a nigger doing in a suit?"

As if he'd read the uniform's mind, Warneke said, "First guy cracks wise, write him up. We'll toss him tomorrow."

"Yeah, but—"

Warneke was going to Zengelman's office near the Paramount.

"You buy the kid the suit, Ben?"

The old man was shaking, and Warneke wondered why it hit him so hard.

Zengelman stared a hole in the blotter under the gooseneck lamp. Contracts were stacked in a wire basket, bills clipped to envelopes, and the drawers of the khaki cabinets were labeled to reflect perfection in filing. A meticulous office, even if the furniture and the green window shades were out of date. Photos signed by celebrities lined the walls.

"Ben. The suit?" It was quiet in the building; across the street, the Paramount marquee was dark.

Zengelman looked up at the cop. "A suit?" he said finally, his voice a hoarse croak.

Warneke came to learn what's new with the kid, thinking it's a race killing, what with the freedom riders and the protests in Bed-Stuy, urban renewal. But Zengelman with his silence said something else.

"Ben, you got a rip. By the collar."

Zengelman's hand went to the shoulder of his vest. Usually, the old man was a pain in the ass, but not tonight.

Warneke sat, his chair in the shadows. "You going to tell me?"

Zengelman said, "I lost a good boy. A sure thing. Voice like an angel."

"OK. But what else?"

Warneke couldn't help but see the stack of 45s near the Victrola.

"What?" Zengelman said. "There should be something worse than that?"

"They're going to fall," Warneke said, nodding toward the records. "You pull one from the middle, Ben?"

Zengelman turned his chair, stood and went to the Victrola. Soon, the black vinyl was set in a seamless column.

Warneke had his hat on his knee. "Junior say something to you? A threat?"

"No. But why? A sweet kid. Not an enemy, as far as I know."

"You had plans for him."

Suddenly animated, Zengelman said, "You know Anthony Gourdine from Fort Greene? Little Anthony and the Imperials?"

Warneke said no.

"Better, this kid. Eugene Pitt? With the Jive Five? Better."

"Ben."

"Brooklyn's Sam Cooke: Junior Maddux, so help me God. Junior—"

"Ben. You're selling me a dead boy."

"With a proper orchestra…" he said, his voice soft again. "Five pieces couldn't keep up, not even Sam Taylor."

"Don't let it grow cold, Ben," Warneke said, as he twirled his hat in his hands. "A ticking clock is nobody's friend."

"I wish I could help," Zengelman replied as he sat.

Warneke stood. "As for who threatened you…"

"Threaten what?" Zengelman gestured with both hands. "They can steal my memories?"

"Ben, your shirt's torn too." He pointed. "The vest, all bunched up The guy grabs with the left, and what's in his right hand?"

Zengelman didn't reply.

Walking away, Warneke said, "Don't make me come back hard, Ben."

"Dialing seven numbers for a couple of days," Warneke said. "Can you do it?"

Warneke favored Perry Como and the Mills Brothers, but his old partner Lanz kept up with the new sounds. Lanz, who made it through Korea playing cornet in a USO band; Lanz, who used to book talent for the annual PBA dinner-dance, putting himself in the combo. Which is how Warneke met Zengelman in '52.

Warneke figured Lanz stepped on the nail on purpose, trying to make disability so he could play music full-time. But Joe Bfstplk since the day he was born, he winds up with tetanus and soon it's too late for Kildare. Warneke would've said it served him right, but he couldn't bring himself to scorn a one-legged cornet player, a guy who kept a folding chair in front of the Dumont.

"Run it by me again," Lanz said. Then he burped, wiped his lips with the back of his hand.

Warneke grimaced. "Schaefer or Rheingold, Joe? I can't tell from here."

Lanz pointed to his fire escape where a case of Rheingold quarts soaked up the morning sun.

"Always a couple in the icebox."

"Plus the one you had for breakfast," Warneke said.

Lanz balanced against the kitchen sink. Warneke tried not to look at the space beneath his pants cuff where an ankle and foot were supposed to be.

"Who's paying? The department?"

"We're kicking in. The Erasmus boys."

"Even though the kid's colored? Man…"

Warneke rapped a knuckle on the plastic tablecloth. "I'll be back by seven," he said. "It's still brisket, isn't it?"

Lanz nodded as he hopped toward his guest. "Your Sheila's?"

"If you earn it," Warneke said, stepping around the cat.

Six days later and Warneke had nothing, like he told Althea after the funeral, back at the Maddux house. Racial harmony, though: everybody heartsick over the loss of this kid.

Leaving his kitchen now, peeling a tangerine, he noticed his daughter's bedroom door open. Liz, ten years old; two, three years from now, she'll loathe the air he breathed, but now she didn't mind he lived. They shared a little joke now and then, and he laughed when she lectured him, wagging a finger, calling him Manny.

She kept a radio on her desk, WINS, and he knew she wrote down the names of the songs. A budding obsession, and maybe he contributed to it: Three years ago, he took her to the Army Terminal, the 382nd Army Band playing "Tutti Frutti" and there's Elvis on the gangplank of the USS *General Randall*, shipping out. Liz said Private Elvis looked right at her when she waved, sitting up there on her father's shoulders.

"What's that?" Warneke asked, standing with his body in the hall, his head in his daughter's room.

"It's so fab," she said excitedly, pointing to the radio. "It's Vince and the Palomars. From Bensonhurst."

"That's Vince Palone?"

She put her fingers across her lips, and she closed her eyes, swaying.

Warneke sat on the chenille spread, guilty when the bed squeaked. Palone was a punk, and he'd turned eighteen in Spofford, the juvenile detention center up in the Bronx. Warneke searched his memory and found it: a couple years ago, a knife fight at the Loew's Oriental; Puerto Rican kid took twenty-seven stitches, but he wouldn't finger Palone.

"Vince Palone?" Warneke repeated when the saxophone ended and the Raceway Park commercial started up.

"It's dreamy, isn't it?" 'Brenda, My Star.' Just a test pressing, not even a real record yet."

"That big loopy guy you made me take you and Finnerty's daughter and what's her name to see at the Bop House? Vince Palone."

"We went for the Tokens. But, yep, Vince and the Palomars."

Warneke thought, Palone had a voice like a cracked foghorn and suddenly he's silky smooth?

"He'll be Brooklyn's Dion," she said, without explaining.

Warneke scratched behind his ear. He had it now, gift-wrapped. Everything but the bow.

"It's going to break national, Manny. Take it to the bank."

Warneke brought Lanz with him, making him strap on the wooden leg. Warneke on his hands and knees, looking for a matching shoe while Lanz brushed his teeth over the dirty dishes, humming the Rheingold jingle.

Now, they stepped out of the rattling elevator.

"Ben!" Lanz said, as he opened the office door.

Zengelman started to smile, but then stopped, and Warneke knew it had occurred to him why they'd come.

Two hobbling cops, and Warneke took the chair on the left, putting his fedora on the desk. Lanz kept his straw porkpie on the back of his head.

"Got any work for me, Ben?" Lanz asked.

"Still in the union, Joe?" Zengelman's stock reply to Grade B musicians.

Warneke saw the old man had his spine back. Not shriveled, and no longer contemplating a mausoleum in Cypress Hills. "Ben, this 'Brenda, My Star'—"

"You heard? Every day in the funny papers you're reminded. Brenda Starr, girl reporter. Mark my words, we're talking here a monster. The Sullivan show! Next week, with the official release on the Laurie label—"

"By Vince and the Palomars. Vince Palone, who sings like I'm shifting into third without the clutch."

Zengelman folded his hands on the blotter. "The recording studio is a house of miracles, Detective."

Lanz said, "Excepting I can't find nobody who seen Palone singing with Sam the Man on sax."

Zengelman frowned. "I don't—"

Warneke said, "You told me Junior Maddux couldn't be contained by a five-piece combo—"

"Drums, bass, piano, guitar, and horn," Lanz counted. "These guys, doing six, seven sessions a day, and the singers roll in, roll out, and nobody notices unless it's some doll. But Manny says you mentioned Sam The Man, so I asked the guys why's Sam Taylor in New York, blowing on some sweet thing in 12/8 time. In D major, modulating to E-flat major out of the bridge."

Warneke rarely used his notebook, but he produced it now for effect. "The Broadway Recording Studio, 1650 Broadway in Manhattan, and Althea says Junior went by subway and you gave him the tokens. A thirty-cent investment, round-trip."

Zengelman was resolute. "The poor woman is mistaken."

Warneke said, "Joe tells me Taylor was back in town for two days. Maybe you called in a favor? They tell me you put him with Alan Freed…"

"A hell of an outro," Lanz added, nodding. "Sam played gorgeous."

"I have no idea what you're—"

"But," Lanz said abruptly, "your Vince Palone looks like a gorilla and Vince Palone sings like a gorilla, and not even Basie in his prime could make that work."

Zengelman drew up. "He's taken lessons—"

"From who? Mario Lanza *and* Billy Eckstine?"

"And his looks, well, there's a certain earthiness the girls find—"

"Ben, in case you need a little nudge, I came up with a Palone composition. Turns out I'd heard him murder it at the Bop House."

Warneke cleared his throat to read Liz's scroll.

"Tonight is the night and the stars are in flight/We'll stroll under beams of moon/We'll take in a show/To the movies we'll go/And then I'll croon you this tune."

"A syllable short," Lanz noted, "unless he goes 'croo-oon.' Or 'too-oon' maybe."

Warneke continued, "Then suddenly this: 'I long to hear you say my name/Whisper as you rest in my arms/To wake in the warmth of your sweet embrace/My dear Brenda." He paused, shutting his pad as he said the last line, "Brenda, My Star."

"Goosebumps." Lanz.

"No, not bad for a sixteen-year-old," Warneke nodded.

"You're mistaken," Zengelman said. "First, Palone is twenty-three—"

Warneke cut him off. "Ben, either you're in or you're out."

Lanz said, "The charts is a funny thing, Manny. Very greasy on the way down."

Zengelman said nothing, but Warneke saw he'd begun to calculate.

The cop stood, checking to see if Lanz needed his elbow.

Zengelman slid his chair from the desk, and he stood too.

Warneke said, "He's going throw away everything for that one last shot."

"Hell, yeah," said Lanz, making sure his phony foot hit the linoleum right, heel to toe, tapping it twice. "Telling Laurie it's that gorilla on vocal…"

"Ben, I break that Palone kid in 15 minutes, but I can't make him for murder. He's knows the game. "

Lanz looked at his partner, watched as his thumb flicked the red feather on his hat held chest high.

"Think it through, Ben," Warneke said. "How's this thing end?"

Warneke found him not in Bensonhurst, but on Mermaid Avenue, outside Tortonno's Pizza, surrounded by little kids in T-shirts and scuffed shoes, and sweet girls in their early teens. Palone was soaking it in, thinking who he was with his pompadour, black Banlon, and pegged slacks, black also. Cuban heels. Reflected on his wraparound sunglasses was the bright Coney Island sky.

Looking, Warneke saw Lanz and Zengelman were almost right, both of them. Palone was half an ape, sure, but he had a bit of a swagger, some of that ring-a-ding-ding. At least in the eyes of the newly minted Our Lady of Solace graduates, and the kids who ran his errands: Palone, rehearsing his star moves on babies.

Warneke stayed by the black Plymouth, called Palone with a crooked finger.

Palone looked this way, that, and then he came toward Warneke, trying to glide, the kids watching.

"Those the Palomars?" Warneke asked, nodding toward the gaggle.

"They're at work," the big man answered.

"Not you?"

"I got to take it easy," he replied. "We've got shows to do. TV, maybe."

"When 'Brenda, My Star' is released."

"On the Laurie—"

"Yeah, I know," Warneke said. "The Laurie label, like Dion and the Belmonts."

Palone pointed at the detective, and he made a clicking sound with his teeth.

"Seems like you've been going at this thing forever," Warneke said, "and now you get your shot."

"I've been working real hard."

"I know. Taking lessons. Good for you, Vince."

The boys watched with curiosity, but the girls were thinking maybe it was time for the beach. A cop talking to Palone and suddenly the towels rolled under their arms were growing heavy, and they remembered they had their bathing suits on under their clothes. Boys their own age were waiting in the sand.

"So what happens next? You ditch the Palomars?"

Palone hesitated. He knew the cops were going to talk to him sooner or later. But this approach he didn't get.

Meanwhile, he noticed Warneke kept peering down at his spit-shined boots, Cuban heels, not exactly a casual glance.

"You change personnel if you got to."

"'Personnel,'" Warneke repeated.

"It happens," Palone replied. "That's show business."

"Zengelman tell you that?"

"As a matter of fact…"

"Anyway," Warneke said, "seeing as you're about to hit the big time, I've got a favor to ask you."

Palone pushed his sunglasses down his bumpy nose and raised an eyebrow. "A favor?"

"You being one of our own."

"I don't—"

"Listen, Vince, if you're thinking of that thing at the Flatbush Hobby Shop? And that time you and what's his name at the Loew's Oriental, the twenty-seven stitches? Let's say it's forgotten."

Palone couldn't put it together. Caught boosting an Aurora model kit when he was eight, he went back and tried to burn the place down. A dozen years later, the switchblade and the Puerto Rican at the movies. Maybe fifteen beefs in between and Warneke says it's forgotten?

Jesus Christ, it's true. Everybody loves a star.

"What can I do for you, Detective?" Palone asked, all puffed up.

Zengelman was no fool, and he came up with the out, if reluctantly. Warneke nodded, not letting on that he'd put it together the same way himself, with Lanz as the sounding board. Lanz, using a knife and fork. Lanz, who said, "Jesus, Manny, it ain't so bad, living."

Palone stormed into Zengelman's office not long after he stomped Junior Maddux, and he went to the pile of 45s, dug out the test pressings and found Junior's demo, "Brenda, My Star." Breathing fire, soaked with sweat, Palone lifted the old man by the shirt front, and he said, "I made this. Me." His right hand a fist, trembling in anger. "And you keep your fuckin' mouth shut."

Warneke didn't have to, but he told Althea the whole thing, and she agreed to the tale: Zengelman would go to Laurie, tell them it was Junior who made the record, Junior who was murdered because the song was so beautiful. Front-page news, "Huntley-Brinkley," Life magazine, and Laurie gets its hit, but without a follow-up. As a kicker, Zengelman throws Laurie half his points on publishing so when Junior's star fades, they can peddle the song to anybody they'd like, Zengelman suggesting Sam Cooke.

Althea said fine. She said Junior had written a bunch of songs, lyrics anyway. Warneke suggested she talk to Lanz, who had a way with melody.

Back home, his wife's borscht burbling on the stove, Warneke made the call, already knowing Palone would bite.

"The favor I mentioned?" Warneke said, checking if Liz was listening. "You don't have to bring the Palomars. Keep the spotlight on yourself, if you know what I mean."

"Yeah," Palone said over the pizza-parlor din. He figured he was getting his picture taken with the mayor, sign some autographs, some civic thing. Wipe the slate clean, like Warneke said.

"As far as Zengelman goes…"

Palone said, "He don't have to know everything."

"No, he don't."

Warneke drove, Palone wearing a tux, looking like a waiter, eleven o'clock on a Thursday morning in mid-August, sucking on his teeth.

"Where're we going?" Palone asked, his elbow out on Flatbush Avenue as they passed the side street where he stomped Junior until he died.

"You'll love this," Warneke replied, as he drove toward the extension.

He turned on DeKalb and put the Plymouth in the cobblestone alley behind the theater. An ancient guy in suspenders and a belt let them in.

"Welcome to the Brooklyn Paramount," Warneke said, stepping aside, letting Palone lead the way through the maze of ropes and pulleys, cables and electrical wires. Stairs going up and more stairs going up. Musty air and the scent of old wood too.

Following, his hand on banisters, Warneke's head was even with Palone's broad ass, but he kept talking.

"A dream come true, no?"

Palone thought, Not without an audience. But with that tune, it's coming, and there'd be more. What did Zengelman tell him? Yeah, the recording studio is a house of miracles. Microphones with echoes built in, background singers, strings. Like that.

Meanwhile, Warneke was studying the bottom of Palone's shoes, looking for dried blood on the taps.

They emerged backstage, and maybe twenty yards away in the vast space was an enormous velvet curtain.

Warneke saw Palone staring up at the gigantic movie screen, craning his neck to look way, way high.

"You ready?" Warneke asked.

Palone had in his mind photographers, politicians, and maybe they brought some screaming kids. Publicity, glad-handing, that shit. He ran a comb through his hair, making a duck's ass.

Warneke signaled for the curtain to open, and it did with a whir and groan.

Palone was greeted by more than four thousand empty seats, and then a lone spotlight from above the second balcony hit him, and he instinctively covered his eyes with his arm.

Warneke looked down at the dozen uniformed cops he had in the front row, and others in the aisles.

"Go," Warneke said, nudging him across raw wood, toward the footlights.

Palone hesitated, and then went forward.

"Vince, say hello to the entertainment committee of the Police Benevolence Association's annual dinner-dance," Warneke said.

Palone looked around, trying to figure. But Warneke was right behind him, and he didn't look too amused.

"You ready?" That was Lanz, sitting at the upright. Every jazz man, no matter his instrument, knew how to play some piano, and a stroll in D major was a piece of cake.

"Sing it, Palone," Warneke spit, legs spread, as the cops in the front row stood and inched toward the orchestra pit. "Sing us 'Brenda, My Star.'"

Lanz played the four-bar intro, as Warneke slipped his handcuffs from his side pocket.

Right is Right
By
Gabriel Cohen

RIGHT IS RIGHT
GABRIEL COHEN

DOWN IN THE BASEMENT, IT TOOK THE repairman ten seconds to figure out what was wrong with the washing machine, and two minutes to make it worse.

A scrap of towel was wrapped around the base of the central agitator. That was the only problem, but the man cocked his head and listened for the lady of the house, who was gabbing away on the phone upstairs. He pulled out a screwdriver, opened the back of the machine, and removed the motor.

Upstairs in the attic, I watched on a surveillance monitor as he stuffed the part into his toolbox. I guessed that he would take it out to his truck, exchange it for a burnt-out one, then sell the woman her own motor back as a replacement. The house was an old brownstone; he'd figure that she could afford it. I grinned as I pantomimed casting a fishing rod, then reeled it in. *"Boom boom boom,"* I sang to myself, *"another one bites the dust."*

A couple of minutes later I turned toward the monitor that covered the front hall and watched as the lady of the house, my partner from Consumer Affairs, paid the repairman and got him to sign the bill. The guy was basically autographing his own warrant, but we couldn't bust him now; we didn't want word to get out about our little operation.

A moment later, Elena Vazquez appeared in the doorway of our chilly attic office. "Well, that one was a real dirtbag."

I nodded.

"How'd I do?" she said.

"You were great. A real Meryl Streep."

I watched the woman register my complete lack of enthusiasm. She evidently decided to shrug it off.

The hell with it, I thought. She'd been frosty with me from the get-go. Spending time alone in the house the way we'd had to for the past three days, I could see why she might want to maintain a bit of distance, but I could have reassured her. She wasn't my type.

Later, after she went home, my boss dropped by. NYPD Detective Sergeant Harry Weinstein glanced at the log: five visits for the day, two dirty repairmen caught on tape.

"Nice job," he said, picking up a copy of the Yellow Pages. "If you can maintain your cover, we'll work this for every appliance guy in here. Maybe we can even move on to plumbers."

"Gee whiz," I replied. "How about chimney sweeps?"

Harry raised an eyebrow. "You being sarcastic?"

"You got me going after *washing machine repairmen*, Harry. I was making Mob cases."

My boss shrugged. "It's not my fault you got into that mess."

"What do you think I should have done?"

"I don't know, Frank. I think you should be glad you're still working at all."

I bit my tongue at that, counted to ten like they had taught me in the mandatory anger management class.

"How long you been with Consumer Affairs?" I asked Vazquez as we sipped our takeout coffee the next morning.

"Three years."

"You ever work a sting before?"

"No. Have you?"

"Plenty. You've never done *one?*"

She just stared at me in her irritatingly patient way.

"So, how'd you get on this job?" I continued. "No offense—I'm sure you're qualified and all—"

She stood up. "I have to go down and reset the towel."

⚜

In the middle of the afternoon we had some downtime between repair visits. The woman read the paper as if it was the most interesting thing in the world. Far more interesting than chewing the fat with ole Frank Monte.

Suit yourself, babe. I turned on the radio, cranked up a Jets game, waited to see if she'd have the nerve to ask me to turn it down.

⚜

During the next appointment, I watched on the monitor as she let the repairman in, did her housewife act. She was convincing, I had to give her that.

I bumped up the magnification. Actually, she wasn't a bad-looking woman. Nice olive skin, pretty brown hair, though she always wore it up. A cute little nose, its tip shining under the hall light like a pearl onion. Not much in the cleavage department, though—or so I guessed. I had to; she dressed like a nun.

I scoffed at myself: I was supposed to be watching *the repair guy.* This one was a geezer in a belted jumpsuit, a little old *papi.* The Mexicans dominated the streets on the west side of nearby Sunset Park. On the east, it was Chinese.

Brooklyn, a broad flat plain covered with tribes.

⚜

When she returned to the attic, the woman looked troubled.

"What's the matter?" I said.

"Nothing. I just felt kind of sorry for that guy."

"What are you talking about?"

"I don't know. He seemed so nice."

I snorted. "Yeah—that was real charming the way he made up that crap about the burnt-out drive shaft."

"Maybe he wouldn't have done this if we didn't give him the opportunity."

I shook my head. "This is not entrapment. All you say is, 'Can you check out the machine?' He goes downstairs. If he's honest, he comes up honest. If he's dirty, he comes up with dirt on his face."

"It's that simple?"

"Right is right. Wrong is wrong. What else can I say?"

↯

The repairmen kept coming. The dishonest ones had different techniques. One attached a burnt piece of wire to the selector switch, another cut the motor belt. One bold bastard just whacked the motor with a wrench.

Visit number twenty-seven brought unexpected trouble.

I watched as my partner asked about the problem.

"I already fixed it," the guy replied. Not a big man, but he had the beefy, bloated look of a loser who relied on steroids to impress his buddies at the gym. He took a step forward. "I hope your husband appreciates what a fine-looking woman he's got here."

"What do I owe you?" Vazquez said quickly.

"How about a little kiss?" The repairman moved forward, crowding her against the washing machine.

"Shit," I muttered, hoping I could get to the basement before some real unpleasantness went down.

I found Vazquez standing above the repairman, who knelt on the floor, clutching his groin.

She turned. "This is a repairman, honey. He had a little accident."

After the guy left and we tromped back up to the attic, I gave my partner a new look of appraisal. Not only had she taken care of herself, she'd managed to maintain our cover. I thought of the repairman's stunned face and had to grin. "They teach you moves like that in Consumer Affairs?"

Vazquez picked up some paperwork, shrugged like nothing much had happened. "They taught me moves like that growing up in East New York."

☽

I was in a cheery mood the next morning. Why? Who knew? Maybe it was the excellent breakfast special I'd discovered at a diner around the corner.

"Hey, Looocy," I called out as I walked into the attic. "Where's Little Rickie?"

Vazquez scowled up at me. "Is that supposed to be amusing?"

I stopped short.

She shook her head. "You think that's funny, putting down Latin-Americans like that?"

"No," I said, actually blushing. "I didn't mean"—

Elena grinned. "Relax, Frank. I was just kidding."

I blinked, and then I grinned too. "You were kidding? Well, *alright.*"

☽

Near the end of the day, I stood by the window and watched another repairman stroll off down the front walk. I turned as Elena reached the attic.

"Clean as a whistle," she said.

I shrugged. "Whaddaya gonna do?"

She glanced at the clock we had installed above one of the attic beams. "Looks like that's it for the day." She put some things in her purse, stood up, and took her coat off a chair.

I cleared my throat. "Hey, listen, you wanna get a beer before we head back? I know an okay place over on Fourth Avenue…"

She sighed. "Thanks, but I have to get home."

"Ah, c'mon," I said. "We've had a long day. Don't you need to unwind a little?"

"My husband's expecting me."

My eyes widened a little; I couldn't help it. "Husband? You never said anything about a husband."

"Was I supposed to? What about this?" She held up her left hand and its bright gold ring.

I sat back in my chair. "I dunno. I figured that was part of your cover."

She shook her head. She turned just before she reached the door. "Were you ever married?"

I busied myself turning off the equipment. "Nah. I've come close once or twice, but I don't think it's for me."

ᴇ

The next morning I made sure the VCR was recording as another mook pried open the back of the washing machine.

I pantomimed palming a basketball at the foul line. "He shoots! He scores! See ya in court, shmucko." I made a note in the incident log.

A moment later, Elena walked in.

"Very well done," I said. "I give it a nine-point-five."

Her mouth turned up a little, despite herself.

Her cell phone rang. She picked up. "Hi, honey, what's up?" She frowned. "I'm sorry. I'll take care of it as soon as I get home." She noticed me eyeing her and turned away, lowering her voice.

The conversation went on for another minute. Elena practically squirmed in her chair. Evidently hubby was not ready to let go of his big complaint. I started to get a mental picture of the guy: some kind of aggressive, macho Latin. Somebody who enjoyed pushing his wife around.

Elena put a hand over her forehead. "Can we talk about this later?" She hung up and groaned.

I busied myself writing in the log, but I was thinking: trouble on the home front?

⚇

The next day Elena looked tired as she walked in. She glanced at her desk. "Weren't you supposed to buy the coffees today?"

I stood. "I been thinking—why don't we just use the kitchen downstairs? I'm sure the people who're renting us this place won't mind. We can save a lot, not havin' to pay for that damn Starbucks, they can't even call a small coffee a 'small'…"

Downstairs, I had to search through all the drawers before I located a filter for the machine.

Elena leaned against the counter. "It feels strange, spending so much time in someone else's house."

I found a couple of mugs in a cabinet. "I like it. They got a nice setup."

After I brewed some java, we sat at a red Formica table in the corner and I pretended to read an old newspaper. I set it down and grinned. "Kinda like being married, huh?"

She scoffed. "Sure—except we have no bills to pay, no laundry, no future to argue about…"

"You argue about your future?"

She gave me a look. "No offense, Frank, but I don't really want to discuss my marriage here…"

"Sure," I said. "No problem."

We sat in silence until she finished her coffee.

I reached into my pocket, took out my wallet.

"What are you doing?" she asked.

I drew out a dollar and set it under the box of coffee filters.

"Wow," she said. "You're a real Boy Scout."

I shrugged. "Hey, right is right."

⚇

The next afternoon, she painted her nails while we waited for the next repair visit.

I swung side to side in my office chair. "You mind if I ask you something?"

She shook her head.

"What's with the nail thing? Nail parlors, manicures, all that crap. I mean, what's the point?"

She squinted down at her hand. "The point?"

"Are women doing this to get guys? Cause—I could be wrong, but I don't think there are many guys out there that really give a shit, pardon my French. I think the nails just get in the way."

She looked up, amused. "In the way of what?"

I flushed. "You know…opening cans. Typing…"

"Anything else?"

I turned away. "I better line up some more appointments."

☙

That night, at home in my little one bedroom in Bay Ridge, I threw my coat over the back of the living room couch. The thing had a big rip in one of the cushions, but I had never bothered to get it fixed. Nobody was going to see it, or at least nobody whose opinion I cared about.

I peered down into an aquarium over in the corner.

"How ya doin', ya little turtle bastard?" I had given the creature to my nephew for his birthday, but my sister had given it back; said her son was allergic. The thing sat on a log now, barely blinking. I snorted. "You make a hell of a pet, you know that? You don't do tricks; you don't guard the house … Don't feel bad about it, though. Whaddaya gonna do? You're a turtle."

I went into the kitchen and heated up some frozen enchiladas. I had a couple of beers, watched a little tube. And then I reached into my coat pocket and took out a videotape. Fast-forwarded to a point when Elena was standing in the front hall, waiting for the next repairman. I watched her in that private moment when she wouldn't have expected to be taped. Alone like that, she didn't look so uptight. She looked pretty nice.

After a minute, ashamed, I clicked off the TV.

I turned on a Seventies-style chrome lamp next to the couch and sat there for a while, looking around my dumpy bachelor pad, thinking about the years of accumulating overtime, then watching TV alone.

A vision came into my mind, me and Elena sitting on the back deck of a nice little house, with a garden maybe, barbecuing…

↙

"*So*," Elena said as she carried in two mugs of fresh coffee the next morning. "I hear you used to be a real hotshot."

I eyed her warily. "What are you talking about?"

"Harry told me. About your Mob cases and all."

I studied her face to make sure she wasn't busting my chops.

She set my coffee down and then sat at her desk, obviously curious but trying to act casual. "What happened?"

I made a face. "Didn't Harry tell you, when he was dishing up my private business?"

She sipped her coffee. "No, actually. He said it was up to you if you wanted to talk about it. So do you?"

"Do I what?"

She leaned forward. "Come on, Frank. We're partners, right? Tell me what happened."

I stared sourly at the opposite wall. After a moment, I ran a hand across my face and sighed. "For years I was trying to make this one Mob case. You remember Joseph Pollito, out in Mill Basin, that they used to call Joey Pipe? He killed some snitch's whole family."

"What about him?"

"I nailed him for the murders, and then he offered to roll over on some bigger fish. The D.A. wanted the publicity—it was an election year—so he was gonna let him plead it down."

"You didn't like that, I take it."

I made another face. "You don't let a scumbag like that practically *walk*."

Elena stared at me. "What did you do?"

"I walked into a meeting of real big shots, NYPD and feds, and I flipped over this table. I told 'em"—

"Let me guess: *Right is right.*"

I smiled sheepishly.

"Good for you," Elena said. "Did they fire you?"

I shook my head. "Nah. I guess they didn't want me to make any kind of public squawk. But they suspended me for three months, made me go to this bullshit anger management class."

"Oh, yeah?" Elena grinned. "How'd that work out?"

↯

The next morning she walked into the attic sporting a big shiner around her left eye.

"Whoa," I said. "What happened to you?"

"It's nothing."

"Nothing? You look like you went a couple of rounds with Mike Tyson." The thought of someone hitting her made my own fists ball up.

"It was an accident. Stupid. The fridge door was iced up and I gave it a yank."

I leaned forward. "A door, huh? Listen, my cousin used to have a problem with doors. And falling down the stairs, kitchen cabinets… Finally I told her husband that if she had one more 'accident' I was gonna personally take him apart." I pictured Elena's husband again. A macho guy, and big. A wife beater.

Elena gave me a surprisingly soft look. "Thanks for the concern. But it was an accident. Really."

I turned away. Maybe it was none of my business, but I had a powerful urge to give the creep a taste of his own medicine.

↯

That night, I watched Elena on tape again, only this time I wasn't ashamed.

☽

The next morning, I walked in and handed her a small box. "What's this?" she asked.

I shrugged. "Just some chocolates. I was thinking about your eye and all. You know, in case it hurts. These are like homemade; there's this fancy new shop down by the Brooklyn Bridge … "

I was babbling, worried she'd think I was out of line, but she set the box on her desk and gave me a nice smile.

"Thanks."

I felt a pain in my heart, as if some celestial repairman had intentionally stabbed it, and I had to admit to myself that I was falling in love.

☽

The next week was rough.

I did my best to play it cool, to keep things professional, but I started becoming hyper-aware of every little thing about Elena. How she sat, the way she smiled, the times she wouldn't smile, the way I thought I could detect a lingering trace of her scent when she wasn't in the room. All of that crap.

It bothered me. I was acting like some goofy rookie, some dip-shit who didn't know any better. And I did know better, or at least enough not to screw up a good operation for some lame personal reason. I needed to do well on that job, needed it for my career.

Late one afternoon, I listened to Elena and her husband having it out on the phone again. She seemed really upset this time; if she wasn't so tough, I'm sure she would have had herself a good cry. Then I listened as she called up some female pal, asked if she wanted to go and see a movie. I felt jealous, can you believe it?

She left early, because we didn't have any more repair visits. The attic was getting dark fast, one of those gloomy evenings of a seemingly endless winter. I was restless, real restless. After pacing around for a while, too wired to do any work, I got an idea.

⬇

The building was in the South Slope, one of those old warehouses newly converted to condos. The windows were big, but all of the shades were down. I could see into the little foyer, though, with its potted plants and ritzy track lighting. I sat outside in my car. Every few minutes I had to reach out and wipe my icy breath off the side window.

One of my cold hands was wrapped around a little something I usually kept in my trunk: a telescoping steel baton, illegal in New York State, something I had taken off a nightclub bouncer. The more I thought about it, bubbles rising from the hot saucepan of my heart, the better the idea seemed: I would meet Elena's husband out on the sidewalk in front of the building. Forget what they had told me in that course—sometimes a little righteous anger was the proper response. My vision narrowed as I dropped into a full-fledged fantasy: dropping the man with one swing, hearing him plead for the mercy he had not shown his much-smaller wife, swinging the baton and feeling a satisfying connection of metal against teeth, a spray of red…

A yuppie blonde couple came out, all duded up in some kind of fancy running suits, despite the cold. They set off down the sidewalk doing some kind of ridiculous speed-walking thing. What a crock. I turned my attention back to the door: a tall black woman carrying a briefcase. She tucked a cell phone between her ear and her shoulder as she reached into her pocket for her key.

After five minutes, a Chinese takeout delivery guy bicycled up. He wore a very skimpy metallic jacket with epaulets, and I wondered how he did his job all night without freezing to death. Then a slim guy came out, shoulders hunched because of the way both his forearms pressed down on aluminum canes. His body twisted with every step; I figured he had some kind of neurological disease. He was followed by a couple, a stout guy sporting a fancy cashmere coat and a plump Asian woman wearing fluffy white earmuffs.

I scrunched down in my seat, thought about turning on the heater for a few minutes. I hadn't seen anyone who looked remotely like a big Hispanic guy. I knew the address was right, because I had copied it off a utility bill I'd found on Elena's desk.

I was freezing, and I should have gone home, but I stayed on for a while. There was something burrowing inside of me, some bad pain or sadness, and I needed to get it out, to send it into the world as something else.

People came and went, the temperature dropped, my window iced faster. Finally, I realized what a pointless thing I was doing, lurking like some sick skel, and I got out of there before anybody else started to wonder what I was up to.

⚐

The next day, I could hardly look Elena in the face. But that didn't stop me from watching her on the monitors, every chance I got.

⚐

Two days later I was at my desk organizing some paperwork when she suddenly spoke up.

"Oh, look!"

"What is it?" I said.

"It's snowing."

I stood up and joined her at the window. Outside, big downy flakes were falling. The street and the trees were already turning white.

"I love it," she said.

"Looks like our last visit might get cancelled."

"Maybe we should head home before the streets get bad."

"There's no rush," I said. "We're still on the clock, right? We can get paid for watching the snow."

We stood in silence for a couple of minutes. We hadn't turned on any lights, and the room was softly growing dark.

"When I was little," she said, "I came from Puerto Rico. I had never seen snow. I thought it would be warm, like feathers."

"Were you disappointed by the real thing?"

"Who could be disappointed with this?"

After a moment, she sighed.

"What's the matter?"

She shrugged. "Nothing. This is nice."

I nodded. "Yeah."

We were only a couple of feet apart.

I turned to her. Reached out and gently touched her cheek. "Is this okay?"

She closed her eyes, leaned into my hand. I could feel a current running between us, something very strong. We stood like that for another minute.

Until I pulled back. She was *married*. To some loser who hit her, but married nonetheless.

Wrong was wrong.

She opened her eyes. She turned her head. She kissed my palm.

I wanted to put my arms around her something fierce.

"It's okay," she said. "I want to."

I stood there in silence.

I stared out at the snow.

I walked away and picked up my coat.

⚕

The next two days, aside from the business of the job, we barely exchanged a word.

The day after that, Harry Weinstein showed up, said he thought maybe the operation had run its course. The whole time he was there, Elena wouldn't lift her eyes from her desk.

There was one final order of business.

The challenge was to find a way to arrest all of the dirty repairmen at once, so they wouldn't have a chance to warn their compatriots. Harry arranged to borrow a big office downtown, and then I called all the bums and told them that I was with the City Department of Finance, said that they had been overcharged fiteen hundred dollars on their taxes, that they needed to come in person on a certain Friday to collect their refund. Nineteen repairmen showed up, crowing about their unexpected windfall. One by one Harry led them into a back room, where they were officially charged. Most of them tried to bullshit their way out, at least until I played the tapes. Some cursed, some pleaded, one even cried—and then a couple of uniforms from the local precinct hustled them out back to a waiting NYPD bus.

I went about the job like a robot. Elena's awkwardness around me took away the satisfaction I'd been looking forward to for so damned long.

Late in the day, I overheard her talking to her husband on her cell phone. I gathered that the guy was coming by to pick her up.

I thought of the way her soft lips had felt against my palm. Then I pictured her black eye. My forearms tensed. I thought of that steel baton again, sitting in my trunk.

Harry brought in several more repairman, but I could barely focus on the job. With the last guy, I looked up and realized that the man was the old papi from Sunset Park.

"No, *please*," the geezer said as we showed him how he had become a star on reality TV. "My son will never forgive me," he said, panicking. I thought for a minute that the old guy was going to have a heart attack.

I looked into his eyes and saw a fellow human being, a man in pain, just like me.

But he was also a criminal.

And right was right.

✼

Later, after the repairman had been led off to the bus with the others, I sat in the corner of the office, sipping a cup of lukewarm coffee, watching the clock. I had stepped out to my car and retrieved the baton, and it sat heavy in my jacket pocket. I couldn't start anything in the office, obviously, but I could follow Elena's husband back out to the parking lot.

Someone knocked on the door and my fists tightened.

Elena got up and invited the visitor in.

A small guy, about her size. Slim, with thinning hair. His narrow shoulders were hunched because of the way both his forearms pressed down on aluminum canes.

He lurched across the room, smiling a generous, off-kilter smile. "Are you Frank Monte? I'm Hector, Lainey's husband. My wife has told me great things about you." He rested one of the canes against a desk and extended a thin, gnarled hand.

It took me a moment to accept the man's shake. I mumbled a vague hello, then watched as Elena briskly steered him toward the door. Just before they reached it, she turned her head and gave me a quick look that I couldn't begin to figure out.

After they left, I sat slumped in my chair, thinking about how I didn't know much about women, or marriage, or life in general, really.

Then I finished the last sip of my coffee, stood up, and closed the operation down.

THE LAST HONEST MAN IN BROOKLYN
MICHELE MARTINEZ

WHEN THE HEROIN DEALER AND SNITCH KNOWN as Kaboom beeped Detective Jimmy Cepeda to ask for a meet, Jimmy wasn't inclined to waste his time. Not at first, anyway.

"Come out in this mess after the way you played me before?" Jimmy said. Sitting in his nice dry cubicle at the Task Force headquarters, he leaned sideways and looked out the window. It was late August, late afternoon, and raining like something from the Bible. In his office, the air conditioning hummed pleasantly and he'd just poured a fresh cup of coffee. Jimmy wasn't about to walk from the lobby to his car in this shit, let alone drive to Bushwick.

"What you mean?" Kaboom asked.

"I used your information on that stash house warrant and came up empty. I looked like a fuckin' idiot."

"So I'll make it up to you. Listen to this. There's meth getting cooked in Marcy Projects."

"Now I know you're full of it. There's no meth in Brooklyn, period, let alone the Houses."

"That's what everybody think, but they're wrong."

"No way. It's a redneck drug. Stupid white people in the South, one step above sniffing gas. The Dominicans and the Puerto Ricans steer clear of the shit. They got the Colombians to hook 'em up with the real deal, and besides, the Colombians keep the meth out because it screws with their profits."

"You right about that. This chick cooking it up in her bath-room, everybody know it, but the Colombians leave her alone. Why? Wouldn't surprise me if she got protection from way up, like kingpin level, you feel me?"

"A chick cookin' meth in the Houses? Gimme a fucking break." Jimmy was one beat away from slamming down the phone, yet something in this last bit caught his attention. "What's she look like?" he asked instead.

"Get this. She white. White skin, white hair, red lipstick. She look like a ghost, like some kinda movie star ghost. You ask me, that explain the protection. Shorties from the corners coming around sniffin' after pussy and end up taking a taste of product. Now they hooked. She creatin' a problem for everybody."

Jimmy started thinking about this girl he'd seen standing under a street lamp on Myrtle Avenue, must have been about a year ago now, smoking a cigarette. A white girl, platinum blonde hair and red lipstick. Around three o'clock in the morning, and Jimmy'd been driving by in his unmarked G-ride with the heavy tints. Her posture and her outfit told him she was trawling for johns. Vice wasn't even his beat; Jimmy worked narcotics. But he liked clean streets. Besides, she didn't look like any hooker he'd ever seen in that neighborhood before. He'd rolled down the window. *Hello, Detective,* she'd said, so cool, and those sunken eyes. Methed-out eyes, for sure.

"Yo, you heard what I said?" Kaboom asked after a minute.

"Yeah. I'm supposed to believe not only that there's meth but that there's a white chick selling it? In the Houses? Come on." He snorted.

"You think I'ma make this shit up? The bitch causing me prob-lems."

"That why you're dropping a dime on her?"

Kaboom hesitated, but he knew better than to lie about some-thing so obvious. "Fuck, yeah. So? You interested or not?"

"Depends. Marcy Houses got twenty-seven buildings. You got a more precise location for me, or am I just supposed to start busting down doors?"

"Yo, slip me the Benjamins, son. You'll get what you need."

"Let's get something straight. This better pan out. It's your last chance, and I know a lot about you, Kaboom. Remember that. I could lock your Puerto Rican ass up any time without breaking a sweat."

"No worries. You gonna be a big hero, just watch."

"Right. I'm holding my breath."

They made a plan to meet up later that night. In the meantime, Jimmy did what he usually did. Typed out a bunch of overtime requests. Ordered in some supper from the lousy diner across the street. Caught some grief from his group supervisor about how his paperwork wasn't in order for inspection. *Yeah, because I'm the only guy you got who can handle the street. I'm actually out making cases instead of sitting around blowing smoke up your ass.* Ignored three pages and two phone calls from his wife until finally she left him a voicemail busting his balls for not being home the last five nights in a row. After all these years, the woman still didn't get that she was married to a cop.

All the while, he was thinking about that night a year or so back when he saw the girl, how he'd glanced up and down the deserted block before stepping out of his car. How he'd flashed his badge, which she took in with her glazed-over stare. *Can I see some ID, miss?* How she'd held his eyes as she took a deep drag, blowing the smoke right at his face, like a challenge. *I wish I had ID to show you, officer, but somebody stole my wallet,* she'd said. *Too much crime in this neighborhood. Cops don't do shit about it, either.* Brazen little skank. He saw right away what a skank she was. The tattoos, the greenish-purple bruises on her pale arms.He could just imagine how she got bruises like that. But her face gave back light. It glowed. There was even something pure about it. *So what's your name?* he'd asked.

⚜

When Jimmy walked out to his car to go meet Kaboom, it was already dark. The rain had stopped but the city was no cooler, and the steaming sidewalks gave off that familiar summer stink. A little garbage, a little wet concrete, lots of dog piss. You'd think the rain would clean things up, but all it did was bring out the stench.

Jimmy drove out to Coney Island and found a parking spot right near Nathan's, across from the red neon sign that said "KFURTERS." The line was backed up out the door tonight with scum of every shape, size, and color, the whole criminal melting pot, hungry and spoiling for a fight in the heat. Skinny dope fiends, fat made guys, bulky Russians dressed in clothes that'd fallen off the back of a truck. Outstanding warrants on every last one of 'em, he'd wager. Some of the lowlifes checked Jimmy out warily. He looked like your average respectable middle-aged Puerto Rican businessman, in pressed slacks and a nylon polo shirt, but a practiced eye would look at him and read cop. *She* had, she'd seen it before he'd ever stepped from his government-issue sedan. She'd smelled it on him.

They call me Crystal, she said, in answer to his question. *I didn't ask what they call you. I asked your name. And your date of birth, while you're at it, so I can run you for warrants.* She tossed her head. *I know my rights. I don't have to tell you shit.* Bitch wouldn't give an inch. Something fluttered and shifted inside him. For a brief second, his vision went cloudy. He looked around again to check that the street was still empty. *Get in the car,* he said.

As Jimmy contemplated the Nathan's line, Kaboom emerged from inside, wiping some mustard from his mouth with a paper napkin. He crumpled the napkin up and threw it into the pile of soggy, decaying garbage in the gutter. People in the crowd made way for him, a fact which didn't escape Jimmy's notice. Even in this group, Kaboom stood out as one scary-looking motherfucker—dessicated face and a fade haircut that did nothing to hide the ugly lump of flesh that had once been his left ear. That was an interesting little story. Kaboom's ear got bit off by a rottweiler that belonged to a stick-up kid known as Nine, who took Kaboom's drugs and money in addition to his ear. Not long after, Nine showed up dismembered in a trash bag under an overpass of the BQE. Kaboom had an alibi, and Nine had plenty of other enemies. But still, Jimmy had a feeling he could make that case if he tried.

Without so much as glancing in Jimmy's direction, Kaboom strode off toward Astroland. Jimmy stood there long enough to make it look legit, then turned and walked the same way at a relaxed pace. He passed through the gates into the neon carnival, catching up with Kaboom in front of a booth with a sign that read "Shoot the Freak—Live Human Target." The shooting was done with a toy rifle that tripped a lever to dunk the freak in some rancid-looking water. The kid in the wet clown suit sitting on the shelf looked plenty nervous, even scared. You could tell he was thinking that sitting under a sign like that in a place like this was likely to be a losing proposition.

Kaboom stood with his back to the booth, nervously scanning the crowded amusement park. Jimmy stepped up to the window and bought tickets. They didn't acknowledge each other. After a moment, Kaboom shook his head almost imperceptibly and walked away. Jimmy let him go, staying to dunk the freak a few times for appearances' sake. Turned out it was good fun.

Ten minutes' walk down the boardwalk, Kaboom stood in the reeking sand looking out at the span of the Verrazano Narrows Bridge, his white track pants and wifebeater shining in the ambient light. This far from Astroland, nobody else was around, and the crash of the waves drowned out the distant strains of accordion music. Jimmy was beginning to wonder if this was some kind of setup. He approached Kaboom from behind, with his hand on his gun and the pleasant sting of adrenaline in his veins. The thought of putting a few in the scumbag's head flitted through his mind. But then Kaboom turned around, looking serious and businesslike. His famous bling sparkled—a gold pendant, big as a fist, which at first glance looked like a cheerful pineapple but on closer inspection became a frighteningly realistic hand grenade.

"Yo, what's good, Jimmy?" Kaboom said in greeting.

"*Nothing's* fucking good. I'm sweating like a pig in this heat from chasing you down. Whaddaya, planning to blow me out here? What's with the spy movie shit?"

"This meth chick is mad connected. I'm risking by telling, okay?"

"What do you want, a medal? Don't talk then."

"Yo, chill out," Kaboom said, raising his hands placatingly.

"Stop wasting my time."

"All right, all right."

"Where's all this specific information you promised me?"

"Where's my money?"

"With *your* track record? No fucking way. If the information checks out, then you get paid."

Kaboom sighed.

"What's your problem?" Jimmy demanded. "I thought you wanted her dealt with."

"I do."

"So give me the information, and I'll deal with her."

Kaboom suddenly reached for his waistband, and Jimmy drew on him in a flash.

"What the fuck!" Kaboom was breathing heavily, staring straight into the barrel of Jimmy's Glock. He thrust his hands into the air. "You surprise me, son. How long we known each other? Is there no more trust?"

Jimmy gave a deep, genuine laugh. "That's rich, Kaboom. You're good, you know that? So, what're you carrying?"

"Ankle holster is all."

"Keep your hands high and stick your leg all the way out." Jimmy holstered his own weapon. Then, keeping as much distance as he could between himself and Kaboom, he bent down and swiftly removed a small revolver from the holster strapped to Kaboom's leg. Tucking the revolver into his own waistband, he patted Kaboom down, coming up with a money clip containing a thick wad of cash and a Polaroid. He handed the money clip back to Kaboom.

"That's it," Kaboom said, excited. "That's her. Look at the picture. One of my corner shorties took that at a sex and meth party. I'm telling you, right in the Houses and nobody doing shit about it."

"What *is* this world coming to?" Jimmy asked, studying the Polaroid.

It was dark enough that Jimmy had to hold it above his head to see it better in the light blazing from Astroland. He'd been right. It was the girl, Crystal, sitting on a ripped sofa, smoking from a glass pipe, surrounded by several half-naked men. She was naked herself except for a red push-up bra. The table in front of them was littered with pipes and spoons and small baggies of powdered meth. Jimmy stared at the picture for a long minute, then shifted his stance to discourage his stiffening dick.

"What's her name?" he asked Kaboom.

"I ain't got no government name for you, but she go by Crystal, after the drug."

"Looks from this like she moves powder, not ice. Is that right?"

"Yeah. Nobody sell rock, from what I understand. It just ain't necessary."

"You got a building and apartment number for me?" Jimmy asked.

"I don't know where she crib down, but I know where she hang out."

"Your shorty know where this picture was taken?"

"In somebody else's place. That ain't where she cook the shit."

"Cell phone or beeper number?"

"Nothing. Like I said, just where she hang out."

"Okay, where's that?"

"You know that place under the El where they got them drinks Sex on the Beach?" Kaboom asked.

"With the blue sign and the bartender with the little hand?"

"That's the one. But be careful. The bitch mad hooked up in that place."

Jimmy nodded solemnly. "This is looking very promising, Kaboom. I must say, I'm impressed."

"You know I'm always gonna do my best for you."

"This could add up to a nice chunka change for you if it pans out."

"See, what'd I tell you? Meth in Marcy projects. You gonna be a hero."

"I need to keep the photograph."

"No problem."

"You walk out first."

"What about my gun?"

"Like I should hand a concealed carry back to a predicate felon? Get over yourself."

Kaboom glared at him for long enough to make the point but then gave in to the inevitable, turned and walked away. Jimmy watched the white-clad figure recede down the boardwalk until the distant crowd swallowed it up. Then he looked at his watch. It was too early to deal with this problem, so he went to Nathan's and enjoyed a chili dog and fries.

⚜

Around one-thirty, Jimmy Cepeda pushed open the door of the bar under the El. It was long, narrow and dimly lit, smelling of stale beer and bathroom disinfectant. Even at this hour, there appeared to be at least ten people inside, all men, mostly Dominicans and Puerto Ricans, and a few of them checked Jimmy out in a way that troubled him. He was gonna have to put on a show. So he strode right up to the bar and waved his badge at Mini, the bartender, a short Dominican guy whose left hand hung limp and twisted against his side.

Mini could think on his feet. "I don't know who called you, but we ain't got no problems in here, Detective," he said, like he had no idea who Jimmy was.

Jimmy pulled the Polaroid from his pocket. Everyone in the bar was watching him now. "I called myself, my friend. You recognize this girl in the picture?"

The bartender didn't even bother to glance down. "No, sir. I never seen her before."

"Could you do me a favor and actually look at the fucking thing?"

This time, Mini looked. His eyebrows shot up. "No, sir. Her, I'd remember."

"That's odd, because I have solid information saying she turns tricks in your back room."

"I don't know who would tell you a thing like that. I ain't never seen this girl in my life."

"Then you don't mind if I take a look around?"

"Go right ahead. But people get back there all the time and I don't notice if I'm busy at the bar."

"Understood," Jimmy said.

"What you doing?" someone in the crowd called out to Mini. "He ain't got no warrant. He need a warrant."

"Yo, shut up. I ain't risking the liquor license over this shit."

Jimmy glared all around at the patrons and put his hand on his gun as he proceeded toward the back of the bar.

Ten minutes later, after letting the john off with just a warning, Jimmy propelled a handcuffed Crystal through the bar.

"As you were, people. The show's over," he said, as he marched her through.

"You want me call you a lawyer?" Mini asked, but she just shook her head.

Jimmy was parked several blocks away on a deserted side street. When they got to his car, he glanced around, uncuffed her and opened the passenger side door.

When they were both inside, he turned the air conditioning on and sat there looking at her for a minute. She'd gotten dressed in a hurry. The strap of her black tank top was falling off her white shoulder, and her smeared lipstick made it look like somebody'd punched her in the mouth. But her eyes were relatively clear tonight. He liked her like this.

Crystal reached in her jeans pocket for a cigarette.

"Uh-uh, not in the car, you don't," Jimmy said. "My wife'll smell it."

"Okay, so? You don't come around for three weeks and all of a sudden this drama?"

He plucked the Polaroid from the dashboard coin holder and handed it to her. She studied it, her brow furrowed.

"What're you, jealous?" she asked. But then understanding dawned in her eyes. "Who gave this to you?"

"Puerto Rican guy, goes by Kaboom, runs a few dope spots near Marcy Houses. Wears a pendant shaped like a grenade. No left ear."

"Yeah. I think I seen him before. Hmm. What'd I ever do to him?"

"Apparently, you corrupted his crew, took his business." He shrugged. "How should I know what you do?"

She smiled, and reached for her cigarettes again. This time, he didn't stop her. He liked watching her smoke.

"People fucking suck, Jimmy. Don't they?" she said, dragging on it.

"Yup. It's a cruel world."

"So, can you take care of this for me?"

Jimmy blanched. "Jesus, are you kidding?"

"See now, that's why I like you. You're the last honest man in Brooklyn." She laughed, but he felt sick. He was in over his head, and he knew it.

"We never talked about this, understand?" he said.

"Of course not."

"You mention this to anyone, I'll fucking kill you, and I mean it."

She caught his gaze, and licked her lips slowly. "Mmmm, I know you mean it."

He was watching her body. She parked her cigarette in the ashtray and turned toward him. "I owe you now, don't I?"

"It's not that easy, Crystal." He looked away.

"Yes it is," she said, matter-of-factly.

He shifted in his seat, and the movement reminded him that he had Kaboom's gun stuck in his waistband. That wasn't good; it was evidence. He pulled it out and stared down at it. Then he looked up at Crystal, and something suddenly occurred to him. He pulled his polo shirt out of his pants and wiped the gun clean of prints.

"What're you doing?" she asked, and the alarm in her voice sent a delicious shiver through him. Crystal was still afraid of him. God, this was good.

"Kaboom's gun. Whoever shoots him … it would make sense if they used this," he said, and handed it to her. She studied it.

"Okay."

"The things I do for you," he said, shaking his head. "Now how about doing something for me?"

JUSTICE BROOKLYN STYLE

LOCATION, LOCATION, LOCATION
PETER SPIEGELMAN

TERRY BERK SAT UP IN BED AND stared at the white walls. He'd stopped noticing the smell of new paint and sheetrock two months ago, and the hollow footsteps of realtors and buyers in the empty apartments upstairs had been replaced in recent weeks by the thump and slide of movers and boxes. Terry knew it would soon be time to go. Again.

Vic would come by with an address, a key, and another job, and Terry would go forth and do his business. And a little while later, when the construction crews had done theirs—as cheaply and quickly as possible—Terry would roll up his futon and his yoga mat, pack up his weights, and move—probably east again, into a neighborhood soon to be re-christened by the realtors with a shiny new name. Wherever it was, it would be to a basement apartment, dim and near the boiler room—the last unit to sell, or one reserved for the super. And it would, of course, be rent free. Five years ago he'd thought it was a sweet deal—but no more. Vic was coming by that afternoon, and Terry would tell him then: this next job would be his last, and there'd be no basements when he was done. Instead there'd be a big fucking pile of cash.

Terry went to the window, a narrow sideways rectangle set high up on the wall. Through the metal grate he saw parked cars and a piece of wet sky. Rain again.

"Fuck," he sighed.

Cash money, no more caves, and no more of Vic's bullshit either. No more crap about his connections and the auditions he was fixing—for the toothpaste commercial or the deodorant ad; no more blah blah blah about The Gap. He'd been dangling his contacts for five years now, and what had they come to? A few crappy tool catalogs, the flyers for that car service, the walk-on on the shopping channel, where someone spilled coffee on his shirt and cleaned it with a miracle sponge—eight gigs in five years. That wasn't a modeling career, that was bullshit, and Terry was sick of it. Enough was enough, Rita had said, and as usual she was right.

He went into the bathroom and checked himself in the mirror. The abs looked good—really cut—the routine Rita had shown him was doing the job. Too bad Vic never came through on that Speedo ad. Terry ran a hand over his angular cheeks and square jaw. His skin was okay, smooth and moist, and he could wait a day on shaving—give the pores a break. But his color was off and there were shadows under his eyes, and overall he knew he looked like shit—tired and wrung-out.

And why not? He *was* tired—fucking exhausted—from another night spent tossing and turning, and all the time those dreams eating through his skull. They were like the smells of smoke and garbage that clung to him after one of Vic's jobs, but no amount of scrubbing could wash them away. Even in daylight the dreams weren't far off—just behind his eyelids.

They'd started after the very first job, a sagging brownstone on a block that was still Bushwick then—not yet *East Williamsburg*. Three floors plus a basement, eight units and twelve tenants total—*a dozen stubborn pricks*, Vic called them. Not so stubborn when Terry was through, though. He was like the phantom of the fucking opera in that place, and they were happy to get out with the shirts on their backs and the skin on their bones.

Then the dreams. At first he'd just sit up, sweating and panting in the dark with no memory of what had chased him. But with each new job, bits and pieces stuck to him when he woke, like gum to a shoe. The lady in the walker, crying when she found her lock glued shut; the old man yelling when he saw the steaming turd on the elevator floor; the kids screaming at what was left of the cat. The images and sounds got worse with every building, and after the gig on Hart Street, Terry hadn't slept for a week. The smoke, and that old lady—Mrs. Ruiz—gasping…

That was two years ago, and only recently, with Rita, had he found any peace. Only when she fucked him into oblivion, and wrapped her brown legs around him and put his head against those perfect breasts, could he find perfect, empty sleep.

He went to the living room and unrolled the mat. He lay on his back and put his legs in the air, the way she'd shown him. Four sets of twenty-five, and then the obliques. Slow and careful and every day, that's what Rita said. He breathed and counted and thought about her.

It was just three months since the first time he'd seen her, at the gym on Metropolitan Avenue. He thought she was a trainer. She had the body for it, strong and lean, and she had the look: the pricey workout clothes, the tanning-booth tan, and confidence on all the equipment. It turned out she was a new member. She was doing knee raises on the Roman chair when Terry approached her.

"You're not getting 'em high enough," he said.

"I'm working the abs, genius," she laughed. "Anything more than ninety degrees is a waste." She wasn't breathing hard.

They'd gone for drinks the next night, and Terry found out she was a make-up artist. She worked in Manhattan, she said, at fashion shows and photo shoots and sometimes on commercials. When he told her that he was a model, and about his gigs, she laughed in his face.

"I don't know what you call that," she said, the candlelight shining in her black hair, "but it's not modeling." Terry had bristled and tried to explain, but Rita just laughed some more and ran a fingernail lightly on the back of his hand. She fucked him that night for three hours, and left his head empty and his heart clanging in his chest. Then she wrapped those legs around him and pulled him close.

"Right there, baby," she whispered. "I got you now." She smelled like limes, and he slept till noon.

He wanted her every night after that, but she said no—she had early calls and her roommate didn't like sleepovers—so Terry settled for three times a week. And on those nights, welded together with sweat, he told her about his plans and his work and Vic and pretty much everything else. Rita listened in silence, ran her fingers through his hair, and nodded. When she spoke, her voice was soft and intimate in the dark.

She was right about his abs, and right about Vic, and Terry knew she was right about getting out of here, too. Out of this cave, and Brooklyn—out to L.A. Rita had family there, and friends in the business, and Terry knew that with some cash in hand it was the right move. This afternoon he'd explain it to Vic.

He finished the last set, rolled up the mat, and checked the clip in his Sig Sauer.

☆

Vic Ferrer wedged behind the wheel of the Escalade and moved the beast north on Bedford Avenue, pounding his horn every chance he got. He was pissed off, and not just about traffic. He was pissed at his wife for starting again this morning about her retard brother in Orlando, who lost his fucking job for the fiftieth time, and couldn't Vic get him another one. He was pissed at Amber for deciding to get her fucking nails done, and blowing off their nooner. He was pissed at having to drag his ass out of Peter Luger's before the strudel came, and drag through the rain and traffic, up to fucking Greenpoint. And most of all he was pissed at Terry. Fucking Terry, who'd had so much promise, and who lately was such a large pain in the ass.

A gray Jetta stopped short at a yellow light and Vic stood on the break and leaned on his horn. When the light turned green, he rode the Jetta's bumper until it pulled over at Grand Street, and he flipped the bird at the white-faced guy behind the wheel.

When Vic found Terry, five years before, he was squatting in a third floor apartment in Red Hook—just him and the rats in a building Vic had recently taken over. Vic had smacked him and told him to get the fuck out, and he watched Terry's face the whole time, and saw that he didn't really give a shit. That appealed to Vic, who was always looking out for talent, and to whom not giving a shit was one sure sign. He eased up and brushed the kid off, and took him to a diner around the corner. Two burgers and a soda pried loose his story.

He was 16, and he'd been on his own for six months, ever since the meth ate his mother. He was making a living ripping off queers in the toilets in Prospect Park, and he was moving every few weeks to a new squat. Terry was finishing his fries when Vic asked him what he planned to do with his life. To Vic's surprise, the kid had an answer, and nothing Vic expected.

"Commercials," the kid said. "I'm gonna be a model and maybe an actor—but a model to start. My moms said I got the looks."

Maybe to a meth freak, Vic thought, but he kept a straight face. It was true, the kid was tall and built right, and he was handsome enough under the greasy hair, but the eyes screwed everything up. They were a weird, sled-dog blue, dead and hungry at the same time, and who would buy beer or toothpaste from a guy who looked like he might stick a knife in you just to see what it felt like?

Vic nodded slowly. "Well, I know some people," he said, "but this shit takes time. So how about you make some money while you wait?"

The kid was a natural. He was ice cold and tireless, and some of the shit he came up with—that business with the Quikrete in the garbage chute, and setting up that crack whore in the laundry room—Jesus, it was funny stuff. His very first job, he emptied the building in under two months.

It took a long while for Vic to notice the bags and shadows and shaky hands, and when he did, he figured the kid was on something. Maybe booze, maybe horse, maybe even meth—Vic was a big believer in the apple not falling far—but whatever it was, it didn't worry Vic much. The kid didn't slow down any, and the only agita he ever gave Vic was his nagging about modeling jobs. The only agita until Hart Street, at least.

Really, it was bad luck for the kid—some rags and ten years of the *Daily News*, and what should've been a little garbage fire—

smoky, smelly but no big deal—turned into a four alarm shitstorm. And it was just good luck that the arson guys were too stretched or too lazy to look very hard, and that it was only the old lush on the first floor who'd bought it, and that grandma—Rosa Ruiz—and that none of her grandkids were home at the time. In the end, Vic made out okay—the arson guys went away, the insurance settled quick, the rest of the tenants split, and four months later he had a fresh batch of condos to sell. Terry, on the other hand, was worthless for a month—fidgety and muttering like he had the DTs, and even when he got back on the horse, he looked like a fucking zombie.

Vic smiled at the thought, and thought of Amber. *The living dead guy*—that's what she called the kid, even though she'd seen him only once, and then through the smoked glass of Vic's Escalade. But just from that, and the things Vic told her, she'd pegged him as trouble—a burnout, a headcase, an accident waiting to happen. She was still a kid herself, but in the year she'd been his goomah, he'd learned to trust her judgment. She was smart and hard and cold as Buffalo in winter when she wanted to be. He only wished a few guys in his crew were half as tough.

It was Amber who told him what it meant when Terry griped louder about the modeling, and who predicted quitting would be next. It was Amber who saw the squeeze for cash coming, too, and who convinced Vic to deal with this shit before it got out of hand. Fucking Amber—one smart broad, and a mouth like an Electrolux.

Vic missed the light at McGuiness Boulevard, and while he waited he flipped open the cylinder of his Smith and Wesson.

Terry climbed into the passenger seat and Vic pulled away and headed down McGuiness. He had "Welcome to the Jungle" playing and he sang along. Terry watched the rain for a few blocks. Then he gathered his breath and made his speech.

Last job…change of scene…the modeling…severance pay. Vic watched the road and nodded. When it was over, he shrugged philosophically.

"What can you do?" he said. "All good things, and shit. But you're right, you can't do this forever—you got bigger fish to fry." He looked at Terry, and laughed at the relief on his face. "What?" Vic said. "You thought I'd be pissed?"

Terry nodded. "I thought you'd be something."

"Hey, life goes on—and no regrets. We did good shit together: flipped some buildings, made money, brought a better class of people to Brooklyn. You can't tell Williamsburg from fucking SoHo now, thanks to us. And don't worry—we'll work the money out." Vic laughed and turned up the music and drove south and east.

They rolled up to a low factory building and Vic unlocked the gate and pulled into a loading bay. Terry followed him inside, into a large, dim space with wired windows, rows of concrete columns, and a concrete floor under layers of dirt, cigarette butts, beer cans, and used condoms.

Terry turned around and looked at Vic. "What's the job?"

"Sorry, kid" Vic said. "No job today—just layoffs." He pointed the Smith and Wesson at Terry—and lowered it at the sound of footsteps. His eyes went wide.

She was lean and tanned, and her heart-shaped face was framed by a mass of glossy black hair. She came out of the shadows behind Terry, and he turned to look at her and felt his jaw drop. Vic said something, but Terry didn't understand the words. Rita came up beside him and snaked her hand under his coat and pulled the Sig Sauer out.

"What the fuck are you doing, Amber?" Vic said again, and before Terry could say *Amber who* or even breathe, Vic's head exploded in a loud red cloud.

Between the gunshots and the rushing in his ears, Terry couldn't hear himself scream. When he could, he was yelling at Rita, who was crouched over Vic's body.

"What the fuck did you do—I had this covered. What are you doing? What are those gloves—"

The first shot took Terry in the gut. The second was in the chest, and bright red foam came from his mouth. He went down, and she was beside him.

Terry tried to say her name, but only red bubbles came out. Still, she understood.

"No Rita, bebé, y no Amber, cualquiera. Mi nombre es Carmen. Carmen Ruiz." Her voice was soft and intimate. He smelled limes.

He said something else. More bubbles.

"Si," she said, "ella era mi abuelita. She was my grandma."

Terry opened his mouth once more, and a little red wave ran down his chin. Carmen wrapped his fingers around the Sig Sauer and fired a shot into the shadows. She watched his strange blue eyes cloud up, go blank, and close.

"Right there, baby," she whispered. "I got you now."

ALL BLEEDING STOPS ... EVENTUALLY
TIMOTHY SHEARD

TWENTY PROUD BLACK MEN IN FLASHY ORANGE and white outfits
marched in step along Eastern Parkway beating on steel drums, their
bare arms a blur, their faces glistening and rapturous. Long-legged
women in feathery rainbow costumes strutted behind, their hips
rotating, their faces radiant with joy. The sidewalks spilled over with
two million revelers in Brooklyn's own version of Carnival.

Doctor Robert "Red" Stone dropped a foot to the ground and
balanced his Harley, watching the parade. He tapped his foot to
the music, enjoying a brief moment of merriment before the storm
surge of sick and injured came flooding into the hospital. West
Indian Day was always busy in the Emergency Room, like a Macy's
one-day sale. Although in recent years it had been light for mug-
gings and shootings. People were having too much fun to kill each
other. Besides, the cops were under orders not to make arrests unless
absolutely necessary.

He gunned the engine, adding the rumble of the Harley to the
music and song, then rode east past Utica and the parade's staging
area. He turned south, doubling back along Clarkson until he entered the parking lot of Kings County Hospital, where a young
guard gave him a snappy salute. Red looked up at the grand old
brick building as he walked toward the entrance; it was such an
elegant design, like an eighteenth-century French estate. The new
building where he worked was sleek and steel—imagine, the city

had built a state of the art facility for its poorest citizens—but the old structure had the class.

As he approached the ER, Red heard the scream of a siren coming closer. The screeching tires of an ambulance speeding through an intersection told him this was a bad one. He picked up his pace and entered the ER just as the EMTs came barreling across the landing with a stretcher.

Legrand, a young resident, spotted Red. "We got a stab wound to the chest, thready pulse, deep shock. Sounds like a pneumothorax."

"Or a ruptured aorta," Red cautioned, pressing his stethoscope to the victim's chest as they wheeled him into a bay. "Could be a laceration of the heart." He signaled to the unit clerk at the station. "Get the trauma team down here. *Now.*"

Red noted with approval how the paramedics had cut open the victim's shirt and placed a pressure dressing over the chest just to the right of the breastbone. The location was a hopeful sign; a stab on the other side, the left ventricle would have blown. Instant death. Good-bye. The victim was young, male, black, with tattoos on his arms and the backs of his hands. Prison ink.

Pulling down the victim's trousers, Red jammed a large-bore catheter into a vein in the groin while Legrand cannulated the other side. "Get ten units of blood up here and run them in continuously," he said to the nurse. He didn't have to remind Marita, the senior trauma nurse, what to do. Beautiful even in scrubs, she was a pro; battle tested.

Red took a long spinal needle and jammed it in between the lower ribs, connected a syringe and pulled back on the plunger. Bright blood rapidly filled the syringe.

"He's bleeding big time into the thoracic cavity," he told Marita. "Get the saw, I'm cracking his chest."

Marita opened a cabinet door, pulled out the chest tray, and dropped it on a bedside table. Red ripped the sterilized packet open, plucked the pair of gloves at the top of the instrument tray, and jammed his fingers into them. As Red hit the switch on the saw,

Marita stepped behind him and placed a mask with eye shield over Red's face, tying it in back.

The surgeon pushed his hips back slightly, feeling Marita's soft body.

"You do great things for me," he told her. The saw whined. "Legrand, pour some iodine on the chest."

As the young resident squirted a stream of iodine onto the young man's chest, Red pressed the razor-sharp circular blade into the top of the breastbone and ran the saw downward. He made a neat incision, splitting the bone in two. There was no bleeding from the incision—a bad sign.

As soon as he cut through the connective tissue beneath the bone with a scalpel, a sea of blood welled up out of the chest cavity.

"Lost a little blood, there," Red muttered, suctioning blood out of the opening. "Saline irrigation, please," he said.

Marita opened a bottle of normal saline and poured it directly into the open chest. *Plop … Plop … Plop.* A puddle formed on the tiles at their feet. Red's arms, scrub shirt, and visor were splashed with blood.

"Fuck," said Legrand, "how're you gonna control a massive hemorrhage like that?"

"All bleeding stops eventually," Red deadpanned, prying open the incision. "Look." He pointed to a tear in the right ventricle. Blood squirted from the rip in the heart as it beat madly. Red thought of the speed bag he used to hit when he was on the boxing team in med school. The leathery heart was just as tough and took way more hits.

"I need 4-0 suture!" he called. Legrand tore open a suture set and slapped the needle into Red's open palm. Red began to sew through the beating heart as fast as his large hands would move.

A pool of blood ran off the stretcher onto Red's feet.

"Somebody throw towels on the floor or we'll be falling on our ass."

Marita brought cotton towels from the closet and packed the floor. The white cotton quickly turned crimson.

The suturing complete, Red examined the lungs, finding no signs of laceration. He closed the breastbone and sewed the skin together.

As soon as the patient was stabilized and transferred to the ICU, Red went to the on-call room, where he tore off his blood-soaked scrubs and stepped into the shower. His chest, arms and neck were streaked with blood.

"Fucking A," he muttered, running cold water over his long muscular body. Hot water opened the pores; no sense giving HIV a running start. He squirted antibacterial soap over his chest and worked up a good lather. When he was done he stepped out and looked in the mirror for scratches or cuts. There were no breaks in the skin; some comfort, anyway.

Back in the ER, Red irrigated the stomach of a drunk who'd been vomiting up material that looked like coffee grounds. When Marita came and showed him the man's lab results, he leaned in close to her and said, "I want you to test our stabbing victim for HIV. Okay?"

"You need a consent, Red," she pointed out.

"Fuck the consent, this is Brooklyn. I was splattered with blood, for Christ's sake. Use the point-of-care machine and call it an instrument test."

"That trick doesn't fool anybody," she said.

"So you'll do it?"

"Of course I'll do it. But you owe me a ride home on the bike."

"And I always pay my debts," he said. "Next."

※

Two hours into the shift, the resident summoned Red to see a young black woman, who lay on a stretcher moaning softly. Her cocoa-colored face was swollen and discolored, her eyes nearly shut, a bloody dressing taped to the side of her face. "Raccoon eyes," thought Red. He saw that she had been pretty. "I hate when they destroy beauty. Such a waste."

"What did the x-rays show?" asked Red.

Legrand ticked off the injuries. "She has an orbital fracture on the right, nasal bone fractures, her clavicle is broken in two places, and she has a deep laceration along her left cheek."

Red looked with approval at the simple cotton sling securing the girl's arm.

"What about her abdomen? Any sign of internal bleeding?"

"Her crit is thirty-six. I don't think so."

Red lifted the girl's gown and gently probed her belly. The woman moaned louder.

"Does she speak English?" he asked. Legrand confirmed that she did.

"Sorry, honey, I have to examine you." He thumped her abdomen with two flat fingers. "The belly's not taught. Did you get a flat plate?"

"Yes, the x-ray showed no free air in the abdomen."

"Who did this to you, honey? Who beat you up?"

The girl shrugged. "I don't know him."

To the resident Red asked, "What did her rape kit show?"

"Sir?"

"Her rape kit. You examined her for signs of rape, did you not?"

"Uh, no, she didn't tell me anything about being attacked."

Red grimaced. He pointed at the woman's face. "What do you call *that*—a bad makeover?" He bent down closer to the girl's face and said gently, "I'm going to numb up your face and then I have to do a little sewing. Okay?"

The girl raised her hands to cover her face. "No, please, no. It will hurt me!"

"You won't feel it, dear; really. I'm giving you the same anesthetic the dentists use."

He gently grasped her slender fingers in his large hands and lowered them to her side.

"Get me a topical lidocaine on a swab," he instructed the resident. "And get me 5-0 silk, I'm going to do a plastics stitch." To the girl he said, "I'm going to use a special suture that won't leave hardly any scar. Okay?"

"A scar? On my face?" She raised her hands again in defense.

Softly he said, "It will only be a teeny, tiny mark. A little dab of makeup and you'll be on the cover of all the magazines. I promise."

As he sewed the girl's face, he again saw the beauty beneath the trauma, and wondered, as he had so many times, why a gorgeous girl would let herself be abused by a violent man. He doubted that her story about not knowing her attacker, the pattern was too common. Still …

When he was finished sewing, he put his hand gently on her forehead, as if instilling energy and hope into her with a current of pure energy. Promising to check on her later, he went on to the next patient.

↯

Red was washing his hands in the sink when Marita called to him from a gap in the curtains at the young girl's bay. He joined her behind the curtains.

"She okay?"

"Yeah, fine, she fell asleep." said the nurse. "I was going through her clothing, making an inventory, and I found this."

Marita held up a pair of black pantyhose wrapped around a slender object. She unwound the stocking, revealing a slender knife caked with blood.

"*Shit,*" said Red. He bent down and examined the knife. It was a small folding pocketknife, just two blades. He opened the larger blade and measured it with his thumb, making a mental comparison with the laceration in the stabbing victim's heart.

"It's the right size," he said.

"Do you think … ?"

"I'm not paid to think, I'm just a surgeon." He chewed his lip. "Tell you what. Scrape the blood into a sterile specimen cup, it's still not completely clotted, and see if blood bank can type it. Tell them just to type it; don't prepare a unit for transfusion."

Marita looked into his eyes with fire. "I do this *for her*, not for you."

"Okay."

"And *I drive* the bike, you ride."

"Works for me."

Marita reminded him they needed a name and an ID number to run the blood type. Red thought a moment. "Use the number from the dead guy in bay seven. He won't mind."

Marita swabbed the knife and got enough blood for the lab to run.

"What do you want me to do with the knife?" she asked.

Red took it from her and dropped it in a red sharps container. After Marita left the bay he gathered disposable scissors, bloody gauze dressings, and other trash and dropped them into the rigid container until it was full to the brim.

"Hey, Tran!" he called, drawing back the curtain. "We need a new sharps container in here."

"Okay, doc." Tran brought a fresh container into the bay. He unlocked the clasp—all the sharps containers were locked in place so the addicts and pushers didn't steal them for the needles—and set up an empty container.

"They should not put junk in here," complained Tran. Red grumbled and went on with his work. In the morning the container would go down to the pickup room and be sent to a hazardous waste disposal site where it would be melted down into a sterilized blob.

⚐

Halfway through the twelve-hour shift, Red went up to the ICU to check on his stabbing victim. Approaching the cubicle, he saw his patient had a visitor: a big, dark, muscular man seated at the patient's bedside. Red gave the visitor a moment and went to the station to check the chart. "Street justice is a bitch," he mumbled, noting how many units of blood they had poured into the guy.

As he reviewed the patient's vital signs, Red looked up at the color monitor and saw the visitor leaning in to the patient and speaking to him. Curious, Red pressed the intercom switch for the cubicle, covering the microphone with his hand. Barely able to hear the visitor, Red turned up the volume on the speaker and pressed his ear to the speaker.

" … I got the bitch good, bro'. I whipped her black *ass*; she lucky to be *alive.*" Red watched the scene on the monitor in growing horror. "She cut you like that over another *skirt? Don't make no *sense* no *how.* I didn't kill her, though. Too much trouble with the cops, know what I'm sayin'?"

Red released the switch on the intercom and sat back. *Who's the victim here?* He was losing faith in his original diagnosis. It looked like the girl wasn't so innocent. That made Red suspect he'd protected the wrong injured party.

He went to the cubicle, slid open the door, and introduced himself to the visitor.

"This here's my brother, Malcolm," the big man said. Standing up, he towered a good five inches above Red's six-foot frame. "He gonna be all right, ain't he? I mean, he's not answering me when I call his name."

"Your brother lost a lot of blood; his brain was deprived of oxygen. We'll have to wait and see, but he's young and healthy. I think he'll probably be okay."

"You can't say for sure?"

Red chewed another lip. "Look. The patient was seconds away from death. I had to crack his chest and sew up his heart, but I didn't have time to get him to the operating room, so there's a risk of infection. You need to know that."

"You can treat a infection, can't you? You got drugs f' that."

"We have your brother on broad-spectrum antibiotic coverage, and we're watching closely for signs of infection."

Seeing that the brother was reassured, Red left the ICU and returned to the ER.

⭒

Toward the end of the shift, Red pulled Marita aside and told her what he'd heard in the ICU.

"She's still a victim," Marita said.

"You're probably right. I'm kind of sorry I got rid of the evidence. She *did* try to kill him."

"You know the system," Marita said.

"I know. She gets twenty to life for attempted murder and he gets five to ten for assault. Still … "

Marita picked up her bag and slung it over her shoulder. "They got all the justice they deserve. Come on, let's get outta here."

In the parking lot Red handed Marita the key and waited while she mounted the bike. He loved the way her thighs straddled the frame. Climbing on behind her, he wrapped his arms around her and pushed a hand up to cup her breast. She smacked it down.

"Not till we're home."

"Okay."

She turned the key. As the big engine rumbled to life, she enjoyed the sense of power under her control. Marita snapped the bike into gear and roared out of the lot, lifting the front tire off the pavement.

"Nice wheelie," said Red, staying cool.

They retraced his route to work, crossing Empire Boulevard, now strewn with the detritus of the march and passing a street-sweeping machine working the curb. The ghostly appearance of the empty streets made him sad. Red had always pictured himself as a reveler, but knew deep down he was drawn to dark, lonely roads.

"I heard on the radio no shootings again this year around the parade," he remarked. "Isn't that great?"

"We should celebrate. You got any wine at your place?"

"Champagne in the fridge."

"We'll kill the bottle after I pop your cork."

She gunned the engine and raced for home while Red held on for dear life.

BONESHAKER
MAGGIE ESTEP

NICK WOOL WOKE UP AND WISHED HE hadn't. The sun was blasting through the thin curtains and Angela, the upstairs neighbor, was pacing her floor, by the sound of it wearing the wooden platform shoes Nick had noticed her in a few days earlier. Nick appreciated the sight of Angela in her platforms, the way they made her tiny calves taut, but he didn't want to be hearing those shoes pounding his ceiling just shy of eight AM on a bright Wednesday in July.

He stumbled out of bed and limped over to the kitchenette. He'd ripped a muscle in his right leg while hammering up a hill on his bike two days earlier when he'd called in sick to his job cooking at the lesbian-owned restaurant. Figured maybe the injury was comeuppance for letting his bosses down. They were nice girls.

The mice had left pellets on the kitchenette counter and the programmable coffee maker had forgotten to make the coffee again. Nick closed his eyes. Took a few breaths, opened his eyes back up, and stared at the coffee maker. He unplugged it, carried it to the open window, and threw it out onto the street. It was only two stories down but the thing made a racket smashing into the closed lid of a garbage can.

Nick looked left and right down Front Street. It was one of those end-of-the-world streets abutting the southern tip of the Brooklyn Navy Yard. No one had noticed Nick's act of savagery. Maybe Angela had, but she wouldn't mention it anyway. Never did more than nod hello and scuttle away nervously, like Nick was going to try hiking up her skirt and bending her over the banister. Nick wouldn't do that. All the women he'd ever been with had come on to him first. This wasn't always a good thing, just the way things were.

Nick swigged down a can of Coke, then wheeled his bicycle out of the corner where it lived. He ran his hand along the top tube. It was a no-name 56cm aluminum frame he'd bought at a yard sale upstate. He'd outfitted it with Campagnolo components and a set of Mavic Ksyrium wheels. It was aggressive and obscenely fast, its lone flaw the thinness of its aluminum tubing, which made for a rough ride. Nick had come to think of it as The Boneshaker.He didn't care that it rattled his bones, though. It kept him company now that he'd been dumped by his most recent girlfriend, Alma, and he was now thoroughly alone. Nick had no siblings and his mother had died abruptly two years earlier, leaving Nick her toothless cat, Donut. The moment Nick had grown fond of Donut, the cat had dropped dead. Nick had one friend he'd kept in touch with from Brooklyn College. Bill. Bill was an inveterate gambler, though; prone to long mysterious disappearances. He was in the middle of one now.

Nick got dressed, tucked keys, money, and a small flask of carbohydrate gel into the back pocket of his bike jersey, then hoisted The Boneshaker onto his shoulder and carried it down the two flights to the street.

As he stared at the pieces of his coffee maker on the sidewalk, Nick heard a window opening. He glanced up just as Angela leaned out, long brown hair framing her heart-shaped face. Her nose looked red even from that distance.Maybe she'd been crying. Maybe the platform shoes hurt her feet.

"Good morning," Nick ventured.

"What was that noise before?" Angela asked. She was looking from Nick to the pieces of shattered coffee maker on the sidewalk.

"What noise?" Nick asked innocently.

"Never mind," Angela said. She retreated from the window.

This was the most Angela had ever said to Nick. He stared at her window for a few seconds then hopped onto the Boneshaker, clipped into his pedals, and rolled out.

The sun was so intense it hurt.

By the time Nick had ridden the three-odd miles from Vinegar Hill to Prospect Park, he'd nearly been doored by a truck, his front wheel had hit a greasy manhole cover on Flatbush, almost going out from under him, and a pregnant woman had jaywalked on Union, stepping into the street out of nowhere, forcing Nick to veer so sharply to the left that his knee banged into a lamppost. At least the park was relatively quiet. A few people walking dogs. Recreational riders on mountain bikes, joggers, girls on horseback.

Nick pedaled.

By his fourth lap around the park, Nick had shifted onto the big chain ring and was keeping a twenty-five-miles-per-hour pace. Ahead of him, a pack of racers, serious ones by the looks of their carbon bikes and muscled legs, were riding a paceline. Nick sped up and caught them, riding alongside but not really looking at them. A few guys glanced over at his bike. Gave it appraising looks. Figured it was a piece of shit.

Nick accelerated again and passed the racers. Glanced back over his shoulder. One of them had decided to chase him down. Nick slowed fractionally, letting the guy catch him. He was a little guy with monstrous legs. Riding a Colnago. At least six K worth of bicycle. Nick let the guy tuck in right behind him. A few seconds passed, then the guy made his move. Shot out from behind Nick and started flying up the hill. Nick felt himself smiling. He jumped up out of the saddle, sprinting up the hill's final crest to catch, then pass the racer. The guy never caught him again and Nick just kept riding, going around the loop eight more times before finally heading home to get ready for work.

The last thing he felt like doing was going to work. He was bone tired. Sweaty. His torn leg muscle throbbed. He couldn't let the lesbian restauranteurs down twice in one week, though. He got a can of Coke from the kitchenette, swallowed it in a few gulps, and went into the shower.

When he came out of the bathroom, Nick heard Angela, pacing again. He toyed with the idea of going upstairs and asking her if everything was all right. He'd had a roommate once, a nervous girl who'd paced so much she'd worn her shoes down. She'd eventually been institutionalized. Nick hoped Angela wasn't headed that way. She seemed sweet. He didn't want her to be insane.

Nick combed his hair, locked his apartment, and walked the five blocks from his house to the restaurant.

"Morning, handsome," said Barbie, the butch blonde co-owner. Though Barbie did have blonde, Barbie doll-like hair, she kept it cropped short and her limbs were thick and strong. She did not look like a Barbie.

"Morning, Barb," Nick nodded at his boss. Some days he just couldn't bring himself to call her Barbie.

Nick went into the kitchen and got to work chopping and blending and broiling.

Around six PM, Barbie came looking for him.

"There's a lot of cops up by your house," she said.

"Oh yeah?" Nick said. The Farragut projects were a block from Nick's building. There were always cops around.

"I mean, *right by* your house. Something's going on. You might want to go check it out."

"Oh yeah?" Nick started feeling nervous.

It was close to the dinner rush but Barbie said she'd cover for Nick. Nick thanked her. Walked out and up the hill toward his building.

There was an ambulance and at least half a dozen cop cars parked at awkward angles along Front Street. Angela was standing at the top of the stoop, surrounded by cops and paramedics. As Nick came closer, he saw that one of the medics was holding a huge compress to Angela's neck. There was a lot of blood on the compress.

"Nick," Angela said.

He hadn't realized she knew his name.

"Angela," he said, "What happened here?"

"Burglar," she said, "he tried to kill me. Cut me," she pointed at her neck.

"That's awful," Nick said, taking a few steps closer.

"He cut me cause I didn't want him to take my grandma's diamond ring," Angela said, holding up a naked finger where the ring had been, "I think he was gonna kill me but I kicked him in the balls," she said. Her dark eyes were huge.

"I knew it too," she added, "I knew something was coming. I'd been nervous for like five days."

The post-danger rush was making Angela's speech come out rapid-fire and a little high-pitched. "My grandma always said I had a sixth sense. I always know when trouble's coming."

The medics were trying to coax Angela into the ambulance but she was too wound up. She kept babbling at Nick, as if telling him the whole thing would make it go away.

Nick wanted to urge her to go into the ambulance, get her neck looked at. But she was awfully cute with that bloody compress on her neck.

"He climbed down the fire escape into your place and I called the cops, but then a few minutes later I went to my front window and saw him ride off on your bike," Angela added.

"What?" Nick's stomach knotted. He couldn't have heard her right.

"I know you love that bike," Angela said, "I'm sorry, Nick."

Nick had an insane urge to scream at her, ask her how she could let someone steal his bike. Then he wondered how she knew he loved his bike. He realized this meant she'd actually noticed him and thought about him. This cheered him slightly.

The medics finally wrangled Angela over to the ambulance. She gave Nick a sad little wave as she climbed in.

Nick went up to his apartment with one of the cops. There were two crime scene guys in there dusting for prints, leaving black powder everywhere, making a huge mess. Nick figured they probably wouldn't have even bothered doing that much if the thief hadn't almost stabbed Angela to death.

Later, after the cops had left, Barbie called. Nick had completely forgotten to go back to work.

"The guy stabbed a 105-pound girl and took my bike, Barb," Nick said numbly.

Barbie made soothing noises into the phone. Told Nick to take a few days off.

The next day, some cops came and posted police artist sketches of the thief on neighborhood lampposts. Dumb jerk had let Angela get a good look at his face as he'd stabbed her. Nick studied the sketch for a long time. Skinny white guy. Lank dark hair. Pimples.

Nick started having trouble sleeping. He'd be right at the edge of oblivion, then start thinking about The Boneshaker. Wondering how much the guy had sold it for. How the asshole had no idea what The Boneshaker was worth.Then he'd wonder about Angela. If or when she'd come back. He'd heard from Janet, the gossip down the block, that Angela was shaken but okay. Staying at her mother's in Jersey.

Four days after the incident, Nick's friend Brooklyn College Bill suddenly resurfaced. Turned up outside Nick's building one morning, early. Honking the horn on some kind of fancy convertible. A blonde in the passenger seat.

It was early and Nick had been sleeping later and later what with no bike to get up and ride. He wasn't feeling chipper. He put some clothes on and went down to see Bill and his blonde anyway. Didn't want to be an asshole.

"Nicky baby," Bill said, "I hit the Pick Six at Arlington Park. A hundred and fifty-two grand."

Arlington Park, as Nick remembered it, was outside Chicago, Illinois. How Bill had ended up in Illinois, Nick didn't know. He didn't have the strength to ask. Nor did he have the strength to protest when Bill insisted on taking Nick out for a drink. Even though it was nine AM.

The bars weren't open of course, but Lulu, the blonde, had a huge bottle of vodka in her purse. They went and sat on a bench down under the Brooklyn Bridge and took turns taking swigs from the bottle.As Lulu got slobbery and amused herself picking bottles out of the trash and throwing them into the East River, Nick told Bill about what had happened. How the burglar had stabbed a 105-pound girl and ridden off on his bike.

Bill tried to look upset over it but he was riding the kind of high that nothing could pierce. He just got Nick as drunk as possible, then had Lulu sit in his lap in the convertible while he gave him a ride the few blocks to the restaurant for his first day back at work.

"You feeling okay, handsome?" Barbie asked when Nick came in.

"Fine, thanks, Barb," Nick lied. He was drunk and he was depressed and what's more, he had the remains of a hard-on from sitting in Lulu's lap. And he didn't even like blondes.

Nick went into the kitchen and got to work.

Later that day, Bill showed up at the restaurant, asked Nick to come outside with him for a minute.

"It's almost the dinner rush, Bill," Nick said, waving a soup ladle at his friend. He didn't know why Barbie had let Bill into the kitchen. She was usually an ogre about that kind of thing.

Nick went outside with Bill. Lulu was there. Grinning. Probably drunk out of her mind. She was also holding a bicycle. Specifically, a matte black Cannondale R1000.

"It's yours, buddy," Bill said.

"What?" Nick was confused, stared from the bike to Lulu to Bill.

"Not Lulu, the bike. I got you a bike. You were so bummed out."

Nick didn't want a new bike. He wanted The Boneshaker back. He wanted Angela back in her apartment, walking on his ceiling in her platforms.

Nick realized he was acting ungrateful toward Bill, who had just dropped two K on a bicycle. Forced himself to look cheerful. Made appreciative noises. Told Bill and Lulu to sit down and have dinner. It was on him.

Nick wheeled the bike back into the kitchen. Barbie didn't object.

As he worked, Nick snuck glances at the Cannondale. It was a really nice bike. Even the right size. But it wasn't The Boneshaker.

By eleven PM, Barbie had to call a cab for Bill and Lulu, who were way too drunk to drive back to Bill's place in Forest Hills.

Nick thanked his drunken friend some more. Bill vomited on the sidewalk.

After work, Nick went home, took a quick shower, then took the Cannondale for a ride even though it was late. He went to Prospect Park and looped around a few times. The park was so empty.A lone cop posted at one of the transverses. Some young kids on BMX bikes trying to scare Nick by riding full speed toward him. He didn't care, though. Didn't have his Boneshaker to protect. Didn't care if they rammed right into him, knocked him off, took the bike and stabbed him.

The kids veered out of his way at the last minute.

The Cannondale was a sweet ride. But it wasn't the Boneshaker.

It was one AM by the time Nick headed home, riding down Flatbush. He was moving along at a good clip when something caught his eye. He feathered the Cannondale's brakes and turned around, riding up onto the sidewalk to where a white bike was parked. He stared at it. At its beautiful, unassuming white paint job. At the Mavic Ksyrium wheels. At the tiny nick on the chain-stay where a pebble had flown up hard enough to make a dent six months earlier.

It was the Boneshaker. Chained to a signpost like some common commuter bike.

Nick was trying to figure out what to do next when he caught sight of a guy standing at the take-out counter inside the Chinese restaurant.As the guy grabbed his bag of food and turned to come out the door, Nick recognized the face he'd memorized from the police sketches.

Nick hopped onto the Cannondale and pedaled ahead a little ways.

The creep put his bag of Chinese food into his backpack, then unlocked the heavy Kryptonite chain and fastened it around his waist. He hopped on Nick's Boneshaker and started pedaling down Flatbush, passing right in front of Nick.

Nick followed. After a block, he drew closer to the Boneshaker's back wheel. Finally, the asshole noticed. Turned around, looked at

Nick, and snickered. The little creep thought Nick was trying to race him. The guy put his head down and accelerated. Nick stayed on his wheel.

The thief was riding on the far right of the road, Nick a few feet behind him. Nick had suddenly flashed on an image of the pro cyclist Robbie McEwen, a hyper-aggressive Australian guy who, a few spins shy of the finish line in a stage of the Tour de France, had headbutted one of his opponents to try getting his wheel over the line first. Had nearly knocked the guy off his bike.

Nick felt himself smiling. He accelerated, rolled up between the thief and the edge of the sidewalk, and butted the guy with his head, trying to knock him off the Boneshaker. At that very moment, a truck passed by, doing at least fifty miles per hour. The thief, who was leaning far to the left, trying not to fall off his bike, got snagged on something sticking off the side of the truck, was picked off the Boneshaker and then sucked *under the truck*. The Boneshaker was thrown to the sidewalk where it landed soundlessly.

Nick hit his brakes so hard he nearly came over the handlebars. He got off the Cannondale. Ahead, the truck screeched to a halt. Nick stared. The driver had stopped with his back wheel right over the middle of the dead thief's body. The thief's head was twisted at a horrible angle. His eyes were wide and staring up, lifeless.

It was late but there were always people lurking. Dozens materialized now, hungry ghosts creeping from the shadows. Nick stayed frozen to his spot on the sidewalk, about twenty feet from where the people were now gathering around the weeping truck driver and the dead thief.

No one had even noticed Nick.

Nick walked over to the Boneshaker and picked it up. He laid the Cannondale down on the sidewalk where the Boneshaker had been, hopped onto his white bike, and rode home.

When Nick got back to Front Street, he noticed that Angela's light was on. She was back.

Nick went into his apartment and put the Boneshaker in its spot against the wall. He ran his hands all along the frame, feeling for any subtle dents. There weren't any.

Nick brushed his teeth, threw water on his face, then went up to the third floor and knocked on Angela's door.

She was wearing the platforms.

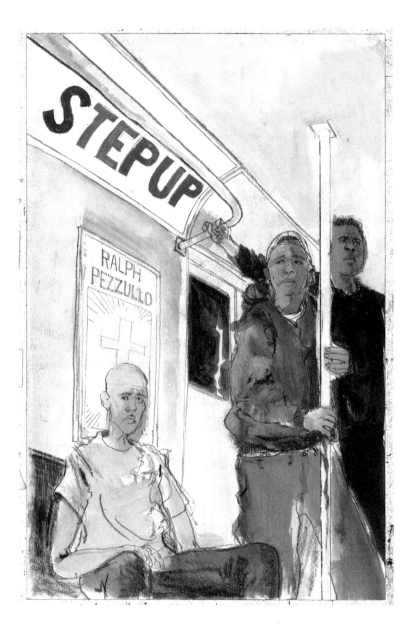

STEP UP
Ralph Pezzullo

DOTEL FELT AS HARD AND SHINY AS stainless steel as the three of them hurtled smooth beneath the streets of Brooklyn—Fulton Street, Eastern Parkway, Church Avenue, south. They were a unit: His cousin K-Mo, Bug-Eye, and him.

"We gotta step up," is all he said as he felt K-Mo's sister Vanna's chicken swirling in his belly with the Dr. Pepper mixed with rum, and greens, two helpings of peach cobbler, and a big scoop of vanilla ice cream. His reflection looked all business in the glass. And he thought of Vanna nursing her baby on the dull green leather sofa with the felt picture of Michael Jordan hovering above her head like Christ.

He thought she'd be proud of him, to see him like this. He was just a few months this side of fourteen, but felt like a man.

Today he'd grown up fast. It started this afternoon when he returned home from school to find Nana, his grandma, slathered in tears on the pink linoleum floor swearing up and down about Reverend Hunter and all the terrible things she was gonna do. At first, Dotel imagined his life swirling down the drain.

Then, the realization smacked him. He had to something. Dotel had left his grandma locked in the bathroom, threatening to slit her wrists.

"Damn," he said, past K-Mo looking out the scratched-up subway window at the flashing blue and yellow lights, past Bug-eye, who was reaching for something in the pockets of his baggy Hilfigers so the plaid boxers he wore underneath slid lower, giving up his ass crack.

Before today, he'd hardly heard Nana swear. Rarely heard her lose her composure. She was upright and strong like the piano that stood in the living room; went about her business; paid no mind to fools.

"What'd Rev. Hunter do?" he had asked.

"The money," she gasped, grabbing at her throat, waving him away with a palm that looked like a big pink pancake.

"What money, Nana?"

"That choir money," she groaned, slamming the door. "He spent it on that ho!"

Dotel might be young and skinny, but he wasn't raised to be no fool. He didn't have to ask: Which ho was that? He knew immediately that Nana was talking about Mistress Tucker with her airs and big white teeth, smiling in that red dress she wore to church with her tits trussed up like balloons.

He hated Mistress Tucker from the first time he'd seen her; she even smelled like bad news.

The story he got through the bathroom door was that Reverend Hunter had taken the money Nana, Mrs. Kaline and them had raised to send the Monroe Street Baptist Church choir to the National Baptist Church Gospel Music Competitions in Saint Louis. Reverend Hunter gave them some mumbo-jumbo about a water bill. But Mrs. Kaline heard that he used the seven thousand to buy another ruby ring for Mistress Hunter.

Everybody knew that Mistress Tucker liked her jewelry. She never missed a chance to shove it in your face. And word through the grapevine was that Reverend Hunter enjoyed the appreciation she showed in bed.

"Your grandma just can't take it no more," she moaned. "This is it! The Lord done tested me one too many times."

"Damn ..."

He loved his grandma. She meant everything—the sun, pretty girls, music, and all that was good in the world rolled together.

She looked after him and his cousins K-Mo and Vanna, and his little nephew, Billy Junior. She made their lives good, cooked them supper, bought them clothes.

All Dotel had left of his mother was a picture of him on her knee at his first birthday party, him wearing a blue matching vest and shorts with a red cone birthday hat on his head.

"Some people ain't prepared for this life," Nana had told him. He understood. He'd learned on the streets that if you don't respect yourself and demand respect from the people around you, you might as well go straight to hell.

"Damn!" It just burned him up to think of Nana, Mrs. Kaline, and all those good women turned inside out by their own Reverend Hunter. How many Saturdays had Dotel seen them, sweating in Nana's little kitchen, baking sweet potato pies and apple cobblers to sell in front of Tompkins Park and raise the money crumb by crumb.

He never did like that church, not that he didn't believe in God and Jesus. He did, deeply. But it made him sad to see all those people hoping against hope, rubbing their knees sore, falling out and praying to their Jesus—the one they felt entering their crowded little basement church—hoping that he was the real Jesus—the one who was the son of God; the son of the God who had kicked them out of the kingdom and let all the Black people fall to muddy earth where they found themselves alone amongst fallen women, tricksters, and sinners.

Despite all the stupid shit he'd done, Dotel's lean heart was pure. His Nana would tell him that at night when she took him in her thick arms and smothered him against her chest. He figured that if Jesus really was strong and good like Nana said, he didn't want people slobbering over him and turning limp.

Tonight he wanted to scream at all the hucksters and the liars who could swipe away an old lady's dignity and hope. He wanted to blow them all away!

He imagined his Nana sitting on her stoop with a jar of wine in her hand, drunk and empty. Reverend Hunter and Mistress Tucker passing in their fine clothes, laughing in her face.

204 HARD BOILED BROOKLYN

Dotel tightened his fingers around the shiny metal pole. The voice cutting through the speaker rasped: "Next stop, Beverly Road."

"That us?" Bug asked like he was waking from a dream, fluttering the long lashes over his big blue-green eyes.

"We're getting out at Courtelyou."

Bug, all five foot one of him, looked up crossed-eyed and cocked his shaved head. He weighed ninety-seven pounds soaking wet. But he had something wild in him that could keep him going night after night without sleep. People said he kept walking the streets because he didn't have a place to stay.

K-Mo was a different story, five shades blacker than Bug and at sixteen, three and a half years older. He was a big boy, ol' K-Mo was, but slow. "Dead-ass slow," his sister Vanna would say. "Like he's some kind a mule pulling the weight of the world behind him."

"We're just going to ask questions," Dotel said so they all understood.

"Yo … "

But Dotel wasn't so sure, drifting off, over the old winos in the park, past downtown Brooklyn, to the river. Manhattan sparkled on the other side like a faraway dream. He imagined himself walking up the Promenade with Vanna on his arm and little Billy Junior, K-Mo, Bug, and Nana all dressed in fine clothes, shading their eyes from the sun.

"This us!" Bug said, slapping Dotel's shoulder.

"Damn." Dotel stiffened up and took a good look at them: himself reflected in the glass, tall but unformed; Bug pulling his mouth, his big eyes blazing with some secret; and K-Mo, a dark, sixteen-year-old time bomb waiting to explode.

It took them less than a minute to meet the concrete walk with Dotel leading the way up East Sixteenth Street under black oak trees that shed big yellow leaves with every gust of wind.

"What we all gonna do?" Bug asked.

"Just you follow me," Dotel answered, feeling that they were heading towards an important moment.

Ditmas Park didn't look like it belonged in Brooklyn with its elegant Victorian-style houses with big yards. Turning left on Dorchester, up two blocks to East Eighteenth, they stopped.

"That's it," Dotel said, looking down at the number he'd written on the underside of the sweatband he wore around his wrist, then up at the big yellow house layered like a birthday cake, glowing under the moon.

"Damn …"

It felt a world away from the two-bedroom flat he shared with Nana, K-Mo, his sister Vanna and Vanna's baby, Billy Junior. From the outside, it didn't look like Reverend Hunter's place had any broken ceilings, peeling paint, water pipes sweating through the walls in summer, roaches climbing out the light sockets and up from the drains.

A lit sign on the front lawn read: Live in faith!

Dotel felt a lump in his chest as he stepped forward, lifted the brass latch on the gate and mounted the thick wood steps to the front door. His heart pounded as he rang the bell, K-Mo dense and dark behind him, Bug jiggling so much Dotel thought he might just blast right out of his shoes.

It happened slow—leaves rattling, then the ding-dong reverberating down the hall, the clock ticking near the front door, the sound of footsteps dragging against the floor.

"Who's that?" she called.

The three of them stood silent. Then he saw Mistress Tucker's big face look out from the curtains, so sure of herself with brown eyes brimming with suspicion.

The door creaked open just a crack and she spoke past the chain. "What are you boys doing here at this hour?"

"We got some business with Reverend Hunter," Dotel said, his mouth turning dry.

"Aren't you Miss Greeley's boy?"

Miss Greeley was his Nana, so Dotel nodded slightly.

"Aren't you Vanna's little brother?" she asked pointing a tapered, red fingernail at K-Mo.

"Yes, ma'am."

Time sped up now and before Dotel could catch his breath, the door was wide open and Mistress Tucker glared down at them in her red silk robe. Reverend Hunter himself came lumbering towards them down the hall with his hands in the pockets of one of those silly jackets white people wear in old movies. He sported a scowl on his wide clown's face.

Dotel was someplace else. It felt like he was in the trees above the house hiding. He couldn't make out what they were saying, Reverend Hunter and Mistress Tucker talking among themselves, tsk-ing and shaking their heads at the boys like they were trash that needed to be swept away.

Dotel heard himself say: "I want my grandma's money." Everything came into focus: the smell of Mistress Tucker's lavender powder, the bourbon of Reverend Hunter's breath, the way the light turned K-Mo's face blue and white, the intricate vine pattern on the rug on the vestibule floor, the veins bulging on the back of Reverend Hunter's hand, Mistress Tucker's big breasts shifting under the robe.

"What?" Reverend Hunter repeated, making the end of the word slide up for dramatic effect. "What are you damn fool boys talking about?"

"The money my grandma and them other ladies raised for the choir. The seven thousand you—"

"Look!" Bug screeched so loud that his voice scraped across the porch and down the street. He was pointing at a big ring on Mistress Tucker's finger with a fancy red stone in it that glittered all kinds of promise. "Look!" he screamed again, freezing everyone in place. Then he reached out his long fingers, took Mistress Tucker's hand like he was asking her to dance and started pulling off the ring.

As soon as she realized what was happening, Mistress Tucker hit Bug with a long looping right that cracked him under the jaw. The crunching sound alone hurt and damn if Dotel didn't see Bug get lifted right out of his Reeboks. But Bug was street, so he didn't let go of the finger. She punched straight in the mouth this time, screaming: "Get off!"

Orange blood poured from Bug's bottom lip onto the front his favorite FUBU shirt. But he kept pulling as Mistress Tucker for screamed for Reverend Hunter to do something. "Call the police, Raymond! Dear God, help!!!!" That's when Dotel saw the knife flash across his body like a bolt of lightning and cut into Mistress Tucker's finger. She threw her head back and screamed so hard that he could see her pink tonsils. K-Mo started using the blade to saw into her.

"Damn …" It pleased Dotel to see Bug and K-Mo working together. Then he heard the bang and smelled the sour cordite. He turned just as K-Mo crumpled at his feet.

Dotel was watching the knife spin through air, when something exploded between his shoulders. His body burned for a second and went numb. He fell sideways in slow-motion through the raw October air and hit the deck hard. K-Mo flailed his legs beside him, blood spurting from a hole in his stomach, spilling onto the wood porch, forming three red fingers that quickly ran to the stairs. "Damn," he thought, looking into K-Mo's blue-green eyes beaming terror and pain.

Three more muffled shots and he felt something moving near his feet. It was Bug going down too. Everything turned soft and mushy. He saw Mistress Tucker's finger with the ring still on it catch the light as it fell onto K-Mo's chest.

He wanted to say: "Cool." Nothing came out.

For some reason the anger inside Dotel faded and so did the yearning and all the needs. He didn't want cars or clothes or anything of that bling bullshit, because he was filled instead with something better, a kind of completeness, a peace, that he had only come close to the first time he had sex.

He glowed from inside—a combination of love, God, Nana, good cooking, family, evenings in summer, and everything that was natural.

"Damn …"

This was what it was all about. And he lay dying. The beams of the porch, yellow leaves, and the stars in the sky turned fuzzy. But Dotel didn't seem to care.

He knew in that one moment that all the suffering, torment, and disappointment of his mean, short life seemed worth it. He had done what he had to do. He had stepped up. He was sure about that. He wasn't saying that what he did was right. Didn't matter. Because he felt a power greater than anything he had ever imagined pulling him towards a place where he knew he would meet his grandma someday and somehow get another chance to love.

GOING, GOING, GONE
Peter Blauner

IT HAPPENS SO FAST. SUSSMAN ONLY TURNS his head for, *what*, maybe two seconds, to check out that hoochie mama in the low-slung ram-riders and the spaghetti-strand top and when he looks back, his six-year-old Ben is already on the Coney Island-bound F train and the shiny metal doors are closing between them.

Sussman pushes through the crowd of departing passengers, trying to pry the doors apart, but it's too late. The train is already starting to move. He runs alongside it, yelling *"STOP"* and gesturing wildly, as Ben stares through the scratchiettied glass in open-mouthed confusion.

But then the window slips past him, like a frame going though a film projector, and he almost collides with a pillar near the end of the platform. A seismic rumble fills the station and he sees the white F on the back of the train receding into darkness, going, going, gone, leaving him stranded.

He pictures his heart untethered from his body, falling through space but somehow still pulsing on its own.

The morning had begun on such a tremulous note of anticipation. This was supposed to be the day when he finally assumed his proper responsibilities and proved he wasn't such a schmuck after all. For the first time since the divorce, he'd managed to get away from work and set aside a full weekend for the kid. No phone calls from clients, no answering e-mails, just *quality* father-and-son time. Up until eleven on Friday night with a Star Wars DVD marathon (which truth be told, he kept watching even after Ben fell asleep two-thirds of the way into *A New Hope*); field box seats from the corporate account at a Saturday afternoon Yankees game (half the innings spent at the souvenir stand, but that's what you get for taking a six-year-old), and dinner at Junior's (three-quarters of a strawberry cheesecake slice left uneaten).

But today was supposed to be the penultimate bonding experience, the maraschino cherry rescued from the bottom of the Shirley Temple glass: the long-awaited pilgrimage to Coney Island that Ben had been begging for. Sussman had been building it up for weeks, telling the kid about the trip he'd make to Astroland every summer with his father, who'd moved the family from Bay Ridge to Long Island back when he was seven. He'd told him about the Cyclone, the bumper cars, the shooting galleries in the midway, and of course, the Wonder Wheel. For some reason, the last attraction had meant the most to the kid; he woke up this morning to find Ben with his crayons in the kitchen, drawing a picture of a stick-figure man running after a spiny Ferris wheel as it rolled down a hill.

Now Sussman stands at the end of the platform, feeling a cold ripple of panic rise from the pit of his stomach. The murmur of the departed train still vibrates through the station.

The only thing that matters. I have lost the only thing that matters. His chest heaves and dread worms into his veins. He looks around—shouldn't there be a station manager on duty or a call box with a button you can push in case of emergencies? But it's still before noon on a Sunday morning in August and the place is desolate. He calls out, "Help," but his voice sounds thin and nasal echoing off the tiled walls. An old bag woman on the opposite platform, her jaw working like Popeye's from overmedication, glares at him furiously, as if she's seen everything that's just happened and knows he's at fault

He starts to run, half-remembering a pay phone he'd once used way down at the other end of the platform for another hassled conversation with his ex. *Yes, I sent the check already. No, I can't take him* next weekend…What will she say about this time? *I knew it! I knew I couldn't leave him alone with you! You're such a fucking thoughtless asshole!* He grabs the phone's gummy yellow receiver, the rusted coil slithers, and then red and green wires spill from the chrome main frame. Broken! Of course!

He drops the receiver in disgust and charges toward the stairs, blood throbbing in his ears. He pictures Ben alone on the train, a wan frightened child in a forest of strangers. Would he think to look for a policeman or another responsible adult? Who knew what his mother had taught him to do in an emergency? He was a fragile kid at the very best of times, and the divorce had shaken him badly. He'd cowered in his bedroom when his parents fought and had turned shy and withdrawn after the split; "a bully-magnet" according to his kindergarten teachers, easily buffaloed away from the more popular toys. Sussman imagines a stranger taking the child's hand and leading him off the train at some unknown stop, saying mommy and daddy are waiting for him there. He leaps up the steps two at a time, the slap of concrete on the bottom of his loafers stinging the soles of his feet.

You're taking your son for the weekend? One of the other guys in sales gawked at him Friday afternoon. *Jesus, I never even knew you'd spawned.*

He stops a second on the landing to catch his breath, his belt buckle digging into a flabby roll. He's terribly out of shape these days, from eating junk food on the road and skipping the gym for weeks on end. *You think somebody's going to give you their account because you're the most relaxed rep they've ever met?* he'd asked one of the newbies just last week. He swallows and sees the token booth a football field and a half away. *No awards for the best excuse. He who hesitates is lunch.* He makes another run for it, his lungs already straining, his knees audibly squeaking. He realizes he's become the stick-figure from Ben's drawing, chasing the giant wheel rolling down the hill. He lifts his thighs and digs for all he's worth. The future has narrowed to this barren gray stretch of concrete from here to the token booth.

But when he gets there the booth is empty. A small beige bag blocks the trench under the glass. For a second, he sees himself like Willem Dafoe on the poster for *Platoon*, falling to his knees as an enemy's bullet rips into his chest.

No. He doesn't even have the luxury of despair. Every wasted second holds the potential for disaster. What's the next stop on the train? His eyes find the map on the wall and start desperately searching for the right artery through Brooklyn. Up until this second, he's never bothered to study other routes besides the ones that take him back and forth to Manhattan.

The wilderness. Though he was born here and has been renting an apartment in Windsor Terrace for two years since the break-up, this borough is still the unexplored wilderness to him. Threatening swatches of Fort Greene and Williamsburg have only been glimpsed fleetingly through car service windows coming home from work late at night. He sees the train cuts through Borough Park and pictures mirthless bearded Hasidim glowering down at his boy. The stops have unfamiliar names like Church Avenue, Ditmas, Kings Highway. He sees "Avenue X," and somehow the starkness of those black letters on the bland beige background strikes terror into his heart.

He runs up the stairs for the street, drenched in sweat, his arteries beginning to constrict.

But the world above ground is oblivious. Just minding its own business and acting like this is just another peaceful Sunday morning on Fifteenth Street, by the park. The sidewalks are empty. Birds sing in the trees. Copies of the Sunday *New York Times* sheathed in blue plastic lie undisturbed on the doorsteps of prim Victorian-looking brownstones and limestones. How can the people upstairs still be sleeping, or having drowsy roll-over sex, or scratching their butts on the way to the bathroom with a hangover, when his whole life is falling apart? How can they be so *complacent*?

He reaches for his cell phone but knows before his hand even touches his pocket that the thing is still sitting on the bedside table, where he'd deliberately left it this morning, so for once he wouldn't be answering calls about work instead of spending time with his son. He imagines it, blinking dumbly, its battery life slowly ebbing away. *Fuck.* Now he can't even call 911. Shouldn't there one of those old-fashioned red Fire Department call boxes on this street? This is a nightmare in broad daylight. This is the beginning of a tragic story in the newspaper. He keeps seeing Ben's stunned little face pulling away from him. His heart squeezes and he feels a dull pain beginning in his left shoulder.

The wheel is rolling down the hill faster, picking up momentum. *Blame.* There must be someone else to blame. It can't *all* be his fault. At work, he's always had a talent for handling pressure and delivering in the clutch, but this is too much for anyone to carry. He pictures Ben surrounded by a roaming wolf pack on the train, a bunch of dead-eyed little thugs demanding the brand-new Game Boy Advance he had with him.

"*Somebody help mee*," his voice joggles as he pounds on down the sidewalk, heading for Eighth Avenue, looking for someone, *anyone*, to make a call for him and stop the trains.

He sees a doughy-looking woman, gray hair sticking out from under a Yankees cap, on her way to the park with a saggy-faced mastiff on a leash.

"Cell phone?" he calls out to her.

She looks at him blankly. The pitch. He has to make a pitch to her, to sell her his terrible need.

"Ex*cuse me.*" He holds his hands out, beseeching. "Do you have a cell phone I could borrow? I'm having an emergency. My child is missing."

She tugs down on the bill of her cap, not meeting his eye as she starts to pass, a time-honored urban tradition for dealing with street crazies.

"Stupid bitch!"

A part of him is appalled, *he doesn't say this sort of thing*, but he can't stop himself. The wheel is spinning out of control. His whole life is on the brink of nullity, of meaninglessness, of total annihilation.

He sees one brownstone without a *Times* on its doorstep and decides the people inside must be awake. Maybe they even have children of their own. He runs up the stoop and starts ringing their buzzer.

"*Hello?*" A groggy female voice comes out of the intercom.

Automatically, he finds himself trying to picture her, like he's making a sales call. He sees a woman no longer young, not nearly old, on her first cup of coffee of the day. The type he could trap on the phone back when he was in telemarketing. He sees her in a flannel bathrobe, trying to make pancakes, moving around the kitchen with a three-year-old clinging to her leg like a little koala bear.

"Hi," he says, trying to modulate and sound reasonable. "I'm sorry to be bothering you. Something terrible has happened. I lost my child on the subway and I need to call 911."

"*Oh.*"

For a moment, time stands still and the wheel stops turning, leaving him suspended at the top of the arc, rocking in the breeze. Everything depends on that one syllable. He tells himself that only someone who's known the joy and pain of childbirth could say "oh" in just exactly that way. Only someone who's stayed up at a feverish child's bedside until the bleak morning hours, with a damp washcloth and a dropper full of Children's Tylenol could draw the word out just so. Only someone who's filled a bathroom with shower steam at three a.m. for a croupy cough could be this empathetic. She understands. She knows he's telling the truth. He's going to close the deal with her. People are good. People are compassionate. This is a borough of neighbors, not a chilly collection of anonymous souls piled on top of each in teetering stacks like Manhattan.

So he waits. And waits. Surely, she'll come back. But then he notices the tightness has moved down his shoulder to his arm now. Where'd she go?

"Hello?" He presses the talk button, knowing she couldn't have forgotten about him. "Are you still there?"

He can almost feel a waft of cool air issuing through the speaker holes.

"For God's sakes, at least make the call for me," he pleads, trying to get her back. "Tell them there's a little boy lost on the Coney Island F train…"

He's wasting his time, he realizes. The deal is off. She doesn't believe him either. No one could be that irresponsible, that criminally negligent, to just leave a child on a train, could they?

He runs for the corner, remembering a bodega there, one of those cramped little twenty-four-hour groceries, where cats chase mice around the produce and disenfranchised men hang around the pay phone outside. The dull pain in his shoulder has become a kind of tourniquet-like tightness. The only thing that matters. I have lost the only thing that matters. All the world could die now and he wouldn't care.

He arrives, gasping for breath, his thighs in flames from rubbing together. But somebody is already at the phone. A trim young man upholstered with muscles, wearing a white silky do-rag and a gold capped tooth that makes him look a little like a pirate. And with him, a girl. But not just any girl. A little sex grenade in a skimpy top and jeans low enough to reveal the jut of her hipbones. The very girl, Sussman realizes, with a sickening clench, he was ogling when Ben got on the train without him.

"Yeah, yeah, but what happened to my tape, son?" The pirate is ranting. "That was my tape, yo…Don't be playing me cheap…"

It's a performance—Sussman sees that right away. The boy is displaying his plumage, showing the girl that he is tough, a defender of his own rights, a man not to be trifled with.

"I'm a kick his ass, he tries to bite me. I'm serious, dawg … "

"Excuse me." Sussman stands before him, gulping, still trying to catch his breath. "I need to use that phone."

"What do you mean, you'll get back to me?" The pirate ignores him. "When does my copyright run out?"

How can anyone be so blindly selfish, Sussman asks himself, so wrapped up in themselves? How can anybody be so unaware there are other people in the world, going through their own private dramas? How can he just automatically assume that his needs are paramount and more urgent than anyone else's?

"I need that phone. *My son is missing.*"

"Say it again, man." The boy turns his back. "Some asshole was trying to talk to me."

Sussman stares at a spot between his shoulder blades, not quite believing what he's just heard.

Force of will, he tells himself. Nothing gets accomplished in this world, without force of will. He sees that every day in sales. Some people just won't move or react until you start to push.

Before he knows what he's doing, Sussman finds himself reaching over the boy's shoulder and pushing down on the pay phone's hook.

"What the fuck?" The boy spins around.

Sussman sees the girl flinch as the boy's gold tooth catches a glint of sun and he knows he's gone too far.

The gray receiver slams into the side of his head. His brain rings as he staggers sideways from the blow. But within the pain, there's something small, hard, and rightful. He knows this is what he deserves.

He clutches at the boy's forearm, to try to keep from falling, but it's too late. His muscles have lost their organizing principle. The back of his head hits the sidewalk. A flashbulb explodes inside his skull.

And in the fading light of the dying filament, he sees Ben alone on the train, drawing that picture of that stick-figure man chasing the wheel, as the Wonder Wheel looms into view against the gray ocean backdrop. It's over now. He's tried, given it everything he had, but he never got ahead of that wheel. It just kept spinning faster and faster, so that he could never catch up with it. And if the boy somehow survives this, his father wonders if he'll just end up chasing the same thing.

Avoid Head-On Collisions.

"Hi, Mrs. Sussman, you don't know me, but I have your son."

The woman in dreadlocks and flip-flops is talking on a cell-phone while keeping an eye on the two small boys as they steer toward each other with the bumper cars, blatantly ignoring the safety sign on the wall.

"Yes, he's fine. I just gave him a hot dog and put him on one of the rides. He gave me your number and asked me to call. Apparently, he got separated from your husband on the train."

She watches the cars crash head-on as the kids jerk back convulsing with laughter.

"Well, I don't exactly know how it happened, but your boy's a real trouper," she says, holding the phone away from her ear a little as the voice on the other end turns sharp. "Some hairy puke started to bother him on the train so he got up and sat next to me because he saw I had a kid. There's grown men don't have that much sense."

The cars skitter and thump across the scuffed floor, barging heedlessly into one another's paths and slamming their front ends together again with joyful abandon.

"Don't worry about it, I'll keep him with me until you get here," she says. "The only thing is, he doesn't know what happened to his father. Maybe you ought to send somebody out to look for him."